Surgeon On The Edge

By

Barbara Jean Quick

DEDICATION

To My Inspiration
As Always

Table Of Contents

Chapter 1

The definition of luck is "to prosper or succeed, especially through chance or good fortune". I hit the luck jackpot when I was an operating room nurse. I was in the right place at the right time. I am a CRNA, which is a Certified Registered Nurse Anesthetist. It is a wonderful career and there is never a day that I hate going to work. My name is Stella Marie Richards Pearce. My mom named me for her favorite aunt, who was a happy and laid-back person and I was blessed with the same easy-going nature. When I was a baby, my dad started calling me his sunny little girl. Like many family names, it stuck. Everyone I know calls me Sunny and most people don't even know my given name. I grew up in a middle-class family in a small town in Southern Michigan. My dad had Crohn's Disease and needed multiple surgeries through the years. I spent a lot of time around hospitals as a kid and developed an early interest in anything medical. My parents were adamant that I get a good education, so they struggled to send me to private school. It was the best gift they could have given me.

When I was a senior, my friend, Pat, used her dad's car for a Friday night out. It was March and the weather was awful. She was worried about driving in such bad weather and suggested that we just go over to the public high school where they were having a dance. I had never been to that high school and was having a great time. As we were walking around, she spotted someone she knew and called him over. "Sunny", she said with a laugh, "I want you to meet the richest guy in town. This is David Pearce." The tall, slim, pleasant guy started laughing and hugged her. "Our families have been friends for a long time" she said. I can't begin to count the number of times I would look at David and scoff "Richest guy in town, hah. Why am I still working?"

He had graduated the year before, but came back occasionally to see old friends. David's father was a local car dealer and a businessman with many investments. He was very successful and the family had been well off. Unfortunately, he had passed away suddenly two years before at age 55. He made the mistake of not teaching his wife about money management and investments. David's mom had never written a check before he passed away. She was a wonderful, loving woman who focused on the home. Her whole life was her husband, children and siblings. She knew nothing about business and had no idea how to deal with business partners. She was not a savvy investor or landlord. In just a few years she was nearly broke. After watching his mother's struggles, David went to school and became an insurance agent. He took many classes in investments and finance. After he got his license, he went to work for a major company and was very successful. He was low-key, honest and people trusted him.

He was heartsick that his knowledge came too late to help his mother save his dad's legacy. He did, however, manage to help her into a more comfortable position for the rest of her life. Following the brief meeting at the dance, David and I started dating.

Chapter 2

After graduation, I went to nursing school. I was very excited about being a nurse because that was just the beginning. There are many avenues open to you once you are an RN. Your clinical rotations help you decide which branch of nursing fits you. I decided to get my Bachelor of Science in Nursing degree, so I would be prepared for any field that interested me. All of the rotations were rewarding and provided an understanding of each branch of nursing and medicine. I liked the ER, but I was especially drawn to the operating room. The OR suited my personality. Every case was a new experience. You might have four appendectomy cases in a row, but each person is different, and each case is different. It also appealed to my desire for focus and intensity. During the surgery, everyone in the room is focused on only one thing, the patient. However, I did notice that some surgeons seem to think that the focus is on them. As I neared graduation, I decided I wanted to become an OR nurse. By this time, David and I were engaged with a wedding planned. I talked to the OR supervisor and she said she would hire me as soon as I passed my state board and was licensed. There would be a training period of four months and I would need to take call.

Call cases were generally emergencies and they were a different routine than the daily scheduled cases. The whole preparation and mindset were different. Some were urgent and time was of the essence. I discussed it with David because my taking call would affect his life too. His response was his usual one. I should do whatever makes me happy. We had dated for five years and I felt very fortunate to have found this wonderful man. I would hear my friends talk about their significant others with arguing, bickering and breakups then reuniting. None of that was part of our life. We just really got along. If we disagreed, we talked it out and moved on. The graduation ceremony was very moving and I knew in my heart that I would be a good nurse. I passed my boards with high scores and soon after, we had a small but beautiful wedding. We had no interest in spending exorbitant amounts of money on a wedding, but we had a great honeymoon in Florida. I had never been there, but David's family went every year when he was a child. A few times they had stayed long enough that he, his brother and sister had gone to school. He loved it there. We had a great time, but were anxious to get home.

I took first call one day a week and one weekend a month. It was always a crap shoot. You might work the whole day and night, or you might not get a call at all. Everyone took their turn at the long days. I had become a very competent OR nurse. One day, about a year and a half later, I noticed a group of people who were dressed out in surgical attire touring the entire department. They were asking a lot of questions, and speaking to the supervisors. They were being escorted by several members of our anesthesia group. Our hospital was a large teaching hospital with residencies in all surgical fields. There were 12 ORs, a urology suite, obstetrics on a separate floor, and an x-ray suite. The anesthesia group was made up of nine MD anesthesiologists and four CRNAs. It seemed like an intense meeting and I asked if anyone knew what was going on. One of the nurses said she heard they were starting a school of nurse anesthesia, and these were the credentialing inspectors. I didn't give it much thought. About a month later, at a staff meeting, the chief of anesthesia announced that a new school of nurse anesthesia was starting in a couple of months. He wanted all staff members to feel free to ask any questions and hoped everyone would make the four new students feel welcome. They had taken science classes at the local university and would be starting the clinical part of the program. This involved doing surgical cases with supervision and sometimes going to lectures. I didn't pay a lot of attention to the school, but I did like all of the students. They were very focused and attentive to their patients. After a few months, I noticed how much more confident they were. About this time, I was walking to the cafeteria for lunch. One of the anesthesiologists fell in step next to me. "Sunny", he said, "come and have lunch with me". This was a surprise. As we settled in with our food, he told me he had been observing me and thought that I was a good nurse with good instincts. He especially liked that I could think and act fast.

"Have you ever thought of becoming a CRNA", he asked. I said "No, I think it looks kind of dull. I like a busier pace." He laughed and said "it looks that way because you don't know what they're doing. In each anesthesia you are coordinating multiple levels of needs for the patient. Why don't you think about it" he urged. "Talk to our current students and get some opinions from them. Investigate the profession. I think you would be an excellent nurse anesthetist. Also, you know, there are a few perks." "Oh", I said, "tell me about that."

"Well, the hours for one thing. Have you noticed how often the students leave after the cases are done? They take turns for late days, but they're often done by two o'clock. You also get the day off after call." Wow. I thought the hours were definitely better than mine. "The other issue" he said "is salary. "It is considerably more than what you currently make. Think about it, Sunny. We have another class starting soon and we would like to have you." I went back to work with my head spinning.

Chapter 3

I looked at the anesthesia providers differently all afternoon. I couldn't wait to tell David and get his opinion. I was also anxious to do some research on nurse anesthesia. What were they doing and would I like to do this every day? As I delved into their history, I was in awe of the accomplishments of these amazing nurses. A CRNA is a specialized type of advanced practice nurse, who administers anesthesia. CRNAs account for more than half of the anesthesia providers in the U.S. and the main provider in rural America. Male nurses have served patients since 250 B.C. and in 1950 approximately 7% of all nurses were male. That number today is about 12%. The number of male nurse anesthetists today is about 37%. Florence Nightingale ushered in the advent of professional nursing during her work in the Crimean war in the 1850s. Nurses also cared for the wounded on the battlefield during the civil war and assisted the doctors and surgeons. The discipline of nurse anesthesia developed in response to surgeons seeking a solution to the high death rates and morbidity from anesthesia care of the times. Some surgeons saw nurses giving undivided attention to the surgical patient and they sought out their expertise for their patients.

The most well-known nurse anesthetist of the 19th century was Alice Magaw, who worked at St. Mary's hospital, which is now Mayo Clinic in Rochester, Minnesota. Dr. Charles Mayo conferred upon her the title "mother of anesthesia". One of her main achievements was her mastery of the open-drop technique for ether and chloroform. One article documented her administration of more than 14,000 anesthetics without a single complication attributed to anesthesia. Together with Dr. Mayo, they shared their professional excellence in anesthesia and surgery with hundreds of physicians and nurses throughout the world. This was a remarkable accomplishment, considering the lack of monitoring equipment and the limited number of medications available. In 1908 Cleveland surgeon, Dr. George Crile asked nurse Agatha Hodgins to become his anesthetist. As she became very adept at administering anesthesia, she began teaching other nurses, doctors and dentists on an informal basis. In 1914 Dr. Crile and Hodgins went to France to help establish hospitals to provide care to the Allied Forces.

When she returned to Cleveland, she established the first school of nurse anesthesia. She called all of her alumni back to Cleveland and in 1939 formed the AANA, which is now the American Association of Nurse Anesthesiology. This is the certifying board for all nurse anesthesia. This board provides the exam for certification and mandatory continuing education. All programs now require a master's degree. In 2025 entry will be doctorate level. As I read the history, I realized that I wanted to be part of this highly specialized group of nurses. The program at my hospital would take three years. Today nurse anesthesia training programs are highly competitive. At the time I was looking, this was a new program. They were seeking students, and good luck put me in this fortunate position. I have always been thankful.

I was anxious to talk to David. I didn't know how he would feel about me going to school for three years. I would not be able to work, and we had discussed starting a family. When David came home, I suggested we go to dinner at one of our favorite Italian restaurants. It was small and cozy, and I knew we could talk leisurely. I laid out the offer I had received and my research findings. I tried to be low-key, but he knew how excited I was. His response was his usual positive encouragement. "Sunny, you know what you want and how to get it. You have always been this way and it's one of the things I love about you. Do it! You will be great". "But what about money" I asked. "I can't work, except maybe a little at the beginning. But definitely not during the clinical training." "We will hold off buying a house and stay where we are renting", he said. "We can make some cuts in our spending, and if needed, we can borrow money or you can get a student loan". It was sounding better and better. "What about kids?" I asked. "We've been talking about it a lot lately". "Babe, you are 26 and I am 28. I think we have lots of time. Do what makes you happy, and listen to your instincts. They have served you well so far". With David's blessing, I told the chief of anesthesia that I was applying to the school. He was pleased and encouraging. He said he could not promise me a job after graduation, but felt confident that one would be available. I asked if I was obligated to work at the hospital for any length of time after graduation. He assured me that I would be free to work anywhere I chose, after I passed my board exam. I would just need to get a nursing license in whatever state I wished to work. Two months later my university classes started. The studies were intense, but so interesting. Then came the much-anticipated clinicals. There were nine MD members of our anesthesia group and all worked with the students. I learned 9 different ways to do the same procedure. Our hospital was multispecialty and I had the opportunity to do every type of surgical anesthesia. There was a residency for plastic surgery with a large burn unit and this was my favorite specialty. It was very rewarding to see how surgical reconstruction could change someone's life. Cosmetic surgery is not covered by insurance, so very little is done in the hospital. Cosmetic procedures were mostly done in the surgeon's office facilities to keep costs affordable. It was interesting to see that certain personalities attracted a surgeon to a particular field. Many eye surgeons were quiet, conservative and very meticulous to the tiniest detail. Orthopedic surgeons were louder, obsessed with technique and more demanding. The general surgeons were very friendly and easy going. The plastic surgeons were my favorite. They were outgoing, always looking for a way to make something just a little better and in general, very personable. I was always trying new anesthesia techniques and new meds to try to improve the patient experience. I really enjoyed my training and felt very confident in my abilities.

Chapter 4

The years passed quickly, and before I knew it, David and I were getting dressed for my graduation dinner and small ceremony. He came up behind me and said "I have something for you" and handed me a small box. I was very excited and opened it to find a key fob. "Wow. What is this"? He smiled broadly and said, "This is your new SUV that we are driving to Florida". I had been offered a job at my training hospital, but had not formally accepted. "I want us to go to Florida and see if we want to make a move. This would be the time," he said. His company was large and there were opportunities in several cities for him to transfer. I hugged and kissed him and ran out the door to see my new SUV. I knew I would miss the anesthesia department and all of my colleagues, but my husband was beaming ear to ear. We made plans for which cities we would visit and in two weeks we were on our way.

Our first stop was in lovely St. Augustine. We stopped at the local hospital and I found my way to the surgical department. The chief of anesthesia was available and met with me. He was a pleasant man and said he could use a new staff member. The hospital was small and the surgical caseload was what is known as bread-and-butter cases. These are standard routine cases. They did not do neurosurgery, cardiac or pediatric cases and they did very little trauma cases. These more complex procedures were sent to Jacksonville. It would be a great job later in my career, but not now. I knew I needed a busier and larger hospital. I thanked him for his time and we headed south. David was pushing for Fort Lauderdale, so that's where we went. I spent a couple of days looking at three different hospitals. They were large and similar to my training facility. David was very disappointed though. He said the area had changed so much, that he wasn't sure that he wanted to work or live there. It was hectic and rushed, not the more relaxed fun place that he remembered as a kid. I agreed with him and felt the hospitals just didn't have a homey feel for me. I wanted to be part of a team, not a cog in a machine. One thing was gratifying and gave me a feeling of comfort. Every place that I inquired would have hired me on the spot. Employment would not be a problem, and I told David not to worry. Florida was a big state and we would find our niche. I suggested that we look in Orlando and the internet showed several large hospitals. Disney was the big draw for tourists, but there were lots of other interesting things to do and the city seemed inviting. So, we headed north.

I found the Orlando City Medical Center. It was only one o'clock when we arrived at our hotel and I thought if we went to the hospital, I might be able to catch someone from the anesthesia department with time to talk. As I walked into the main entrance, I got a good feeling. The desk receptionist called up to the anesthesia department and someone came down and escorted me upstairs. Everyone was pleasant and friendly. The department was large and the caseload was what I was used to. I met the chief nurse anesthetist and she introduced me to the chief of the department. He asked about my training and background and said he thought I would be a good fit in the department. I got a tour and met several members of the anesthesia group. It felt comfortable to me and with a good employment package, I was getting excited. She said I was hired, pending credential verification and background check. First call responsibilities were about the same as I was doing now. Everyone was friendly and that meant a lot. David was waiting in the lobby and saw me smiling ear to ear as I headed toward him. He knew that this was it. We spent the rest of our trip driving around neighborhoods and talking to rental agencies. We found a lovely older house in an area called Delaney Park. Renovations were almost finished and it would be ready in about a month for rental. David would be able to transfer easily as his company wanted to add an agent to their Orlando offices. The next day he visited the office and met his future colleagues. He was pleased and felt confident that he would fit in.

We headed back to Ohio with a month to get organized. I gave my notice as soon as I returned. We shared our excitement with our friends and colleagues about our planned move. There was a month of cleaning, organizing, deciding, and planning, mixed in, of course, with farewell dinners and gatherings with family and friends. We got the usual "Are you kidding? Florida is full of bugs and hurricanes." Also, "we will hire you back when you come to your senses." We were content with our decision and soon moving day arrived. I drove my new SUV loaded with clothing and personal items.

David drove his car towing a rental trailer loaded with boxes and minimal furniture. I had a week to unpack, settle, and shop before I started orientation. David only had three days before he had to be at his new office. We took our time and the trip went well with just minor hiccups.

We met our landlord, finalized the rental agreement and got the key. He recommended a local place for dinner. We toasted our new home and made to-do lists.

Chapter 5

Orientation for me was fast-paced, but thorough. This was a busy hospital and I was eager to learn the routines and protocols. On my first day, I got my locker assignment and went to check it out. I had been assigned a lock code and could change it to my code choice. I found my locker, but could not get the lock to work. I tried three times and was getting frustrated. I heard a friendly voice say, "Hey, are you breaking into my locker?" I looked up to see an attractive woman wearing scrubs and a hospital name tag stating T. Davis RN and a smaller tag above with Teri written on it.

"I'm sorry. I thought this was my locker. I'm looking for 83" I said. "This one is 88," she responded. "Some of the black is faded on the eight and it looks like a three. Here's yours. I'm Teri, one of the OR nurses." "Hi. I'm Sunny, a new CRNA". "Boy I am glad to see you," she said. "We have been short-staffed in anesthesia for a long time and we really need more help." We drifted into an easy conversation and I knew right away that I liked her. "Do you have a few minutes?" she asked. "I would like to introduce you to some of the nursing staff."

I jumped at the chance. Anesthesia is a specialty, but relationships with other staff members are very important. The operating room is a team effort for every procedure. Each member brings a vital aspect to each case. I knew from my previous experience how important the OR circulating nurse is to the team. I had great respect for how hard and tirelessly these nurses worked. I have seen some anesthesia providers and surgeons treat nurses with sarcasm and disrespect, and I just couldn't understand it. The OR nurse is your biggest asset when you need it, so I cultivated good relationships with everyone, even those with difficult personalities. Some of the nurses who had longevity were a bit salty. They had seen it all and they had minimal use for new people. Once you proved yourself, you earned their respect. They were the ones you really wanted when the patient was crashing and you needed everyone pitching in. At a trauma center that happened a lot more often than you liked. Teri introduced me to several staff members and then went back to her OR. I made my way to the anesthesia department. The schedule was posted and I was assigned to cases tomorrow. I was pleased to see it was plastic surgery cases.

The chief CRNA came up while I was looking at the schedule. My favorite, I thought. I would be doing three reconstructive cases with Dr. Mitchell Jacobs. "He's a doll," she said. "A really good surgeon and easy to work with. You're going to start out easy. The supervisory MD anesthesiologist will be one of the easy- going ones. We don't want to scare you away", she laughed.

I arrived early in the morning to allow plenty of time to see my patient and set up my case. There were anesthesia techs here that did more than I was used to. Here they set up the machine, brought equipment into the room, cleaned up between cases and even brought in some of the standard anesthesia drugs. There were techs where I trained, but they did mostly cleaning and maintenance. I appreciated the help, but I already had a pre-op safety routine for myself. I rechecked everything and probably always would. I had been trained to check the machine prior to every use and never let anyone touch my anesthesia drugs. I made a point to tell every tech that I did not want them to touch my tray and I would clean it up myself. The machine maintenance and restocking were fine, but I wanted to handle all my meds myself. They understood and they said that there were a few in the department that felt as I did. Some of the anesthesia providers had been there a long time and had a comfort zone with the techs. I understood, but that was not for me. I didn't even like to use a syringe that I hadn't opened. I had a system that worked well for me and I was not going to change it.

I went to the holding area and met my first patient. He was a pleasant man who had a very bad scar on his arm from an auto accident. It was tight and it prevented him from fully extending his arm. The supervising anesthesiologist stopped by and I told her my anesthesia plan and patient history. When she left, I chatted a bit to put him more at ease. I took his hand and looked into his eyes. I told him we were together for this procedure and I would not leave him for even a minute. I had always done this with my patients and I felt it was reassuring for them. As I turned to leave, I heard a voice from the door say, "Well, that was very nice." There was a tall, attractive man with curly brown hair and friendly eyes.

"I'm Dr. Jacobs," he said. "I heard I was getting a new gas passer today." I shook his hand and introduced myself. I asked if he had any requests for his patients- antibiotics, whether would he be using local anesthesia, et cetera. He laughed and said, "This is refreshing. No one usually gives a damn what I want. They just do whatever they want. Welcome aboard. I'll see you in a few." The day went well. Mitch, as he told me to call him, was a very competent plastic surgeon and his result was excellent. As the day progressed, I inquired if he did cosmetic surgery. "I do", he said, "but not a lot. The guys that focus on cosmetics have state-of-the-art facilities and don't do a lot of reconstruction. I have an office with just a small procedure room. My love is reconstruction, so I'm mostly in the hospital. Have you met Randy Tanner yet?" I said I had not. "He's building a beautiful new facility with a spa and a big OR. It's going to be top-notch. He asked if I wanted to use his facility for cosmetics when he isn't working and I'm thinking about it. He's a bit flamboyant, but he's a great guy. He has had big plans for a long time and they are coming to fruition." The day went smoothly and I was surprised at how tired I was. I had to get back into my rhythm. I checked the next day's schedule and saw I was assigned to two large chest surgeries. Good. I was ready to get back into the big cases. I would be taking my turn for late days, but not first call for the first month. During my third week, I saw that I was scheduled with Dr. Tanner for an abdominoplasty, which is also known as a tummy tuck. I knew tummy tucks were frequently done in outpatient centers or office facilities, but this patient was a type one diabetic and that was why she was being done in the hospital. I was looking forward to meeting Dr. Tanner. I had heard about him from the staff. Everyone admitted he was a talented surgeon, but not everyone liked him. A few found him egotistical and full of himself, while others thought he was just determined and a go-getter. I would see for myself. As I was setting up my case in the OR and checking over my drug tray, I heard a pleasant "Good morning, ladies. I'm so glad to see that I have the A-team today." Before I could respond, he came over and shook my hand. "You must be Sunny," he said with a big smile, "I've heard about you." "Uh oh", I laughed, "I hope it was good." "I hear not only are you pleasant and fun, but your anesthesia is excellent." I was pleased to hear this, but he was a charmer and could just be flattering me. I could see why many people liked him. He was about six feet tall with dark hair and eyes and very good-looking. He had happy eyes and a friendly, open demeanor.

He walked over and began checking the surgical table, calling out suture preferences and special instruments. A tummy tuck is a procedure to remove excess or loose skin in the lower abdomen. It can be done on anyone, but is often done for women after childbirth or after large weight loss. Frequently, the abdominal muscle separates and needs to be tightened. It is very important to get the patient up and walking after surgery. This helps in preventing blood clots. My patient today is diabetic and that adds some risk. Healing can be delayed and blood sugar levels can be more difficult to control. I like my patients awake, moving and deep breathing right away. Our second case was a rhinoplasty, which is a nasal reconstruction. The patient was a biker whose nose was broken in a fight. Nasal surgery can be difficult. You have a small area to work on and subtle surgical maneuvers can have either good or bad results. Dr. Tanner really showed his surgical skills.

He did it without a wasted movement and it looked great. Each of my anesthesia techniques were different. This was one of the things that I enjoyed about my profession. Every patient and every procedure is different and every one requires its own technique and vigilance. As I was finishing up in the recovery room, Dr. Tanner came in to see the patient. I complimented him on the rhinoplasty. I had seen a lot of them, but he was very slick. He laughed. "It is my favorite surgery. If I could, I would limit my practice to just rhinoplasties." He gave a smile and a wave as he walked out the door. The nurse in the recovery room gave a snort. "Don't get sucked in, Sunny," she said. "Sure, he's good, but he's too smooth for me."

Chapter 6

David and I settled into a comfortable routine and time passed quickly. I really enjoyed my work and meeting so many new people. Orlando is an interesting city. It is younger with more energy than some of the other Florida cities we had visited. Our caseload at the hospital reflected this demographic. We did not do obstetrics or pediatrics because there was a specialty hospital for each on campus. We did every other kind of specialty. I started taking first call and felt pretty confident. Teri and I often worked together and we had become good friends. We really clicked because she was a lot like me. She accepts people as they are and she is always honest. She was from Missouri and had grown up hard. She was one of 5 children and her dad was badly injured when he was in his early 30s. It was a difficult childhood, but she never forgot her roots. She was an excellent nurse. She had an innate ability to comfort and calm patients, and many surgeons requested her for their cases. I liked and respected nearly all of my colleagues. There was one CRNA that I really did not warm up to. Bobby McFadden was a distant kind of guy and very defensive about everything. I heard that he had some drug abuse issues in the recent past and felt that he was always being scrutinized and watched. It was probably true. Florida has very strict rules about physicians, nurses, CRNAs or other health care providers returning to work after drug rehabilitation. Although exact numbers are not known, it has been estimated that about 16% of all anesthesia providers have had issues with drug addiction at some time in their careers. Some are never able to return to the operating room environment. In order for re-entry after rehab, you must have a very supportive anesthesia department. There has to be other staff members to secure your opiates for you and they must observe the disposal of the unused medications. They also observe patient behaviors, dosages, et cetera. It may be a very long time, if at all, before you have a narcotic key. Anesthesia opioids, such as Fentanyl, Alfentanil, Sufentanil, Morphine and several others are excellent for providing anesthesia that is safe and effective, but these drugs are very potent and highly addictive. The suicide rate among recovering anesthesia providers is high. It is difficult to break the addiction, and many people become very depressed after multiple failures. I was stunned when I started hearing about Fentanyl becoming a street drug, so it was no surprise when the death toll started climbing. Fentanyl is a potent anesthetic with a very serious side effect. You can stop breathing. I had heard that Bobby had been through rehab twice and had been back to work for over a year. He was still being observed, but that really didn't have anything to do with why I didn't like him. I thought he was rude and unfriendly, but that could be part of his struggle with overcoming addiction. Some people cut him slack because he had a wife who was not in good health and three kids. It seemed like another excuse for bad behavior, but I was determined to keep an open mind.

I had developed a very nice friendship with Mitch. We would grab lunch often and I had invited him for dinner several times. He and David really hit it off and enjoyed each other's company. I loved his sense of humor. When I first met him, I asked him if he was married. He said no, he was divorced, but he had been married twice. "Once", he said, "for two months and once for four months. I have to tell you; it was the longest six months of my life".

He was a real ladies' man. It was a constant flow of beautiful women in and out of his life. That was his personality. He was just a fun person. He had grown up in Connecticut. His dad was a general contractor who worked him in the field at every opportunity in all weather. Academia seemed much more inviting. Mitch loved building and fixing and was drawn to surgery. He had done his general surgery residency here in Orlando then left to do his plastic surgery residency. He came back and set up practice. He was well-known and well-liked, except for professional jealousy. He loved reconstructive surgery and was very good at it. I really enjoyed his cases.

Most of the surgeons were pleasant and predictable. There are always a few that are more difficult, but that is the same everywhere. There was the angry surgeon. The patient was always a crock. The case was the hardest he'd ever done. The staff was incompetent. The equipment was crap and surgical conditions were never right. It never changed, so you rolled your eyes and feigned sympathy. There was the professorial surgeon. They want to teach everyone in the room how brilliant they are. They like to describe everything, just as it's being done and why. They must show it to you over and over. Pretty soon you knew what they were going to say before they said the first word. There was the whiny surgeon. They never get the right room or the right time. Another surgeon is always getting preferential treatment. They get staff that doesn't like them. They are a victim and administration doesn't respect them. There is the sarcastic surgeon. We had one surgeon that fit the mold to a T. He was a pro with his sarcasm usually directed at the circulating nurse. It was almost an art form. He was an excellent chest surgeon and any staff member would not hesitate to be his patient, but he had his moments. At the end of every case, he would thank everyone in the room except whomever he had chosen to harpoon that day. He would say "You", and point to the chosen one, "have been a tower of strength, an absolute tower of strength. I don't know how I could have done this without you, but I sure would have liked to find out." His target would pretend to be offended, but secretly they just laughed. There were other surgeons who were just mean and cruel. Staff abuse was very common for many years, but that was changing. In years past surgeons were an important revenue source for hospitals, so bad behavior was often tolerated. With the changes in insurance reimbursement, doctors contracting directly with the hospital, and a society unwilling to accept abusive behavior, conditions improved.

A hospital is like a small city. You get to know the locals, the gossip, who thinks they are in charge, who really is in charge, and who can get things done. I had been there now for over four months. We were both settled in at our jobs and pleased that we had made the move.

We made friends both from the hospital and the insurance agency, interspersed with visits from our families. We had decided it was time to start a family. All birth control had stopped, but so far, no pregnancy.

Chapter 7

Work was busy and challenging and I enjoyed it. I had gotten to know Randy Tanner somewhat, but one case made a turn in our relationship. It is hospital policy that all women of childbearing age must have a pregnancy test the morning of surgery. The only exception is if she has had a tubal ligation or a hysterectomy. I was scheduled with Randy for a breast lift on a 35-year-old patient. Her husband had a vasectomy, but the policy was to do a test regardless. Vasectomies have been known to fail. I was reviewing her chart when the circulating nurse from my room came looking for me. "You should come to the pre-op room," she said. She seemed a bit disturbed. "The patient and her husband are very upset. Her pregnancy test came back positive and daddy has had a snip. He is agitated and it is getting tense in there". I told her to inform Dr. Tanner right away and I went in to try to calm the situation.

I told the husband that he should get a cup of coffee in the lounge, take a couple of deep breaths, and relax a bit and I would chat with his wife. He agreed. I sat down with my tearful patient and explained about vasectomy failures. She was just sobbing. There had been some stress in their marriage, but she was adamant that she was a faithful wife. There were no other men in her life and she could not understand how this had happened. I spent time and calmed her down. I did some explaining and she was feeling better. I went to the lounge, found her husband and had the same discussion with him. He admitted that his urologist had told him that he needed to return for a sperm check at a later date. It had been scheduled, but he didn't do it. He got busy and it just was never done. It had been several years and he no longer even thought about it. I encouraged him to call his doctor and get tested as soon as possible to put his mind at ease. I told him his wife needed him very much. We talked a bit more and he was calm. I took him back to his wife and they were both crying and talking about what the future would hold for them. Randy came in and told them the surgery was canceled. As they were preparing to leave, they were already discussing how they were going to tell their children about a new baby. As we were walking away. Randy said, "Sunny, you handled that really well. I hate dealing with these personal issues. It's just not what I do well. Let's get coffee for a few minutes". We became friends on that day. Mitch had told me that Randy and his wife were separated and he was going through a rough time. I thought it might be a good idea to have both Randy and Mitch over for dinner. David had heard about Randy and wanted to meet him. It was a lot of fun. Randy had an interesting past that he shared with us and he was a great storyteller. He talked a lot about his new facility that was under construction. It would be a state-of-the-art office with a surgical suite and a separate skin care spa. There had been delays, but it was getting close to being finished. He asked David to stop by so they could discuss some of his insurance needs. He also asked me to come by and offer my thoughts on the surgical suite design plans. We both agreed to take a look.

Time was passing and still no pregnancy. I was looking and feeling down one day and Teri noticed. I shared my disappointment. She mentioned the possibility that maybe I should see a specialist in infertility. She mentioned Sarah Patel, who she said, was excellent in the field. I had not met her because she worked at the women and children's hospital, but I had heard her name. Teri had been at the medical center for years. She knew or knew of just about every doctor in the area. I had never had any gynecological issues, but I was willing to look into anything. I talked to David that evening and he said he was willing to try whatever was needed. I made an appointment with Dr. Patel.

About a week later, I saw Randy in the doctor's lounge. I asked him when he would be at his office, so I could stop by and take a look at his plans. We were both finished and he said "why don't you stop by today"? I met him at his current office, which was very nice, but a typical physician's office. It was nothing like the facility he had described at dinner. I met his office manager, Pam Bryant and liked her immediately. She was a sharp woman in her early forties with an outgoing personality and very pleasant demeanor. Randy told me that she was his right hand for the nearly five years he had been in Orlando.

When he came to town, he got privileges and took call at almost every hospital in the city. He worked very hard to get his name out. His schedule was crazy, but Pam had kept him organized and the office going. He was doing a lot of reconstructive insurance covered cases because that was what came through the E.R. He did some cosmetic procedures and was steadily increasing the numbers. It is a very competitive market and takes time and money to develop, but the practice was definitely growing. His love was cosmetic surgery and that was his goal with the new center. He said he needed to hire a full-time nurse administrator to run the facility and asked if I thought Teri might be interested. I agreed that she would be the perfect nurse for the position.

He showed me his plans and I was amazed. It would be a fully accredited outpatient office facility with a large OR, a 4-bed recovery room, a small treatment room, three patient consult rooms, his office, a kitchen, a locker room, a laundry, a waiting room and a business office with reception area. There was a private door and that lead to a separate full-service spa and skin treatment area. Wow! It was beautiful and impressive. He said other physicians could use the OR when he wasn't working and Mitch was already interested. It was an aggressive plan, but had great growth potential. He planned to hire a professional marketing firm to get his name out there. He was already busy and known around the city, but he needed professional help to reach his goals. Construction was well underway and he invited me to take a look whenever I had time. His surgical reputation was good and that was the most important aspect of his success.

A couple of weeks later David and I had our appointment with Dr. Patel. She was very positive and encouraging that she could help us get pregnant. The meeting was mounds of paperwork and endless details about all the ways fertility treatments could go. Tests were ordered for both of us. We were to return in three weeks to see where we would start. David was not thrilled with the sperm test, but he was willing to do whatever was needed. That evening we were at home relaxing after a busy day. When the doorbell rang, I actually jumped. It was after 9:00 p.m. and we were not expecting anyone. David answered the door and came in with a visibly upset Mitch. "What's happened", I asked. "I just came from the jail", he said. "Randy is in jail". David and I looked at each other with wide eyes. "Oh my God, what happened?" I asked. "He got a DUI". Mitch said.

"He called me and said his lawyer thinks he can get him out tomorrow. I was so upset that I went to the jail, but I couldn't see him. I am in surgery all day tomorrow, so I can't go to court. I'll call his lawyer between cases and see if he needs bail money or anything". I was stunned. David read my mind and asked, "Does Randy have a drinking problem"? Mitch said he didn't think so, but once he had alluded to having an alcohol and drug issue in college. He didn't elaborate and it seemed like it wasn't serious. I made coffee for us and we sat down for over an hour discussing the potential fallout from this event. David was concerned that this could affect his insurability and Mitch was worried about his standing in the medical community. I was just worried about Randy and what could happen. "You are really a good friend, Mitch," I told him. "He was a good friend to me when I needed it", he replied. "When I came back to Orlando 6 years ago, I had to deal with a lot of professional jealousy. The established plastic surgery community didn't want another plastic surgeon in the area. There was resentment because I had contacts here from when I did my general surgery residency. I managed to piss off some of the old guard, and no one would cover my patients if I wanted to go out of town. They manipulated the call schedule to limit my ability to get patients through referrals, and they tried everything to squeeze me out. Randy came to town shortly after I did, and he immediately offered to cover my patients if I needed someone. He managed to get a lot of call and would pass a few days to me. He was an outsider, so no one saw him as a threat. Before long he was busier than most of them. He stood by me and now I will stand by him." We chatted a while longer and when he left, he promised that he would call me as soon as he knew anything. I thought of Randy. All he had worked for could be in jeopardy from one foolish mistake. Thankfully, there was no accident or injury, however, this could have very far-reaching consequences.

Chapter 8

The next day Mitch found me in the OR and asked if I could meet him after work at Randy's office. He said he was going to meet Pam and see what they could do to help hold it together. I agreed and got to Mitch's office just as he was finishing with his last patient. We headed to Randy's. "What happened today"? I asked anxiously." "He had a hearing and the judge gave him a choice. He could do 30 days in jail, plus fines and costs, or go to inpatient rehab. Randy told me he is lucky there was no record of him talking his way out of a DUI in med school." "I didn't realize that Randy had such a drinking problem," I said. "I don't know if it was alcohol," Mitch answered. "It may have been something else. He said he used Adderall to study and occasionally party coke. The cop let him off with a warning and he hasn't had any more issues. Since he got to town, he's been taking call all over the city and now he's really pushing himself because of the new place. Maybe what threw him over the edge this time was the situation with his wife. She's talking divorce and he knows it could have a big impact on the financing for his project. Plus, he really loves his kids". That is a lot on his plate" I responded. "I hope he can get the help and coping skills that he needs. If the new place lives up to his expectations, it won't be less stress. It will be a lot more." Mitch agreed. "I have had issues in my past, thankfully not addiction issues, but other problems. I remember the friends that stood by me and it means a lot. I will try to help him get through this and back on track. He's a good guy and a good friend. We all do stupid things now and then." I agreed. Randy was a good guy. He had a natural gift for surgery and for patient care. He also had the ability to make you feel that you are special. He gave every patient his undivided attention and really listened to them. In this medical digital age, this was becoming a lost art among many physicians. I could understand why his patients liked him so much and he got many referrals. We arrived at Randy's office and found Pam looking noticeably upset. She was happy to see us and felt reassured that we were supportive. She told us that he was leaving in the morning for a highly respected rehab center in Arizona. It was a facility that specialized in working with professional people. Randy had spoken to Pam after the hearing and she had helped set up the stay. He was angry with himself, embarrassed and very worried. Mitch had assured him that we would find a way to keep it together for as long as he needed. We put our heads together and brainstormed for a couple of hours. Workers on the buildout were already scheduled, so that would go on as planned. Pam would come in as usual and be able to follow the work. Randy had signed power of attorney for her to do change orders. He could wire transfer money between accounts if needed. New patients could be rescheduled and Mitch would see current patients to monitor their progress. Randy had waited for months for a meeting with a great medical marketing firm. Levele Health Care Solutions was a top-notch firm limited to professional clients. Charity Levele, the CEO, was well-known for innovative marketing ideas. The meeting was scheduled for 2 weeks out and Pam was hoping that she could move it back. Randy had worked hard to get her interested and that meeting would have to wait for him. Now we needed a reason for him to be gone for a month. We decided on a story that he had gone to visit friends in New York and had injured his left arm. His right arm and hand were fine, but he could not do surgery one-handed. He had to have therapy for a month and decided to stay in New York. We were satisfied that we had the situation in hand and now it was up to him. By the time I got home, I was drained. David had a drink ready and had picked up dinner. I filled him in on the situation.

Two days later we had our anxiously awaited appointment with Dr. Patel. It was overwhelming. David was devastated. His sperm count was very low and Dr. Patel felt our only chance was in vitro fertilization or IVF. He had a bicycle injury when he was a kid and she thought that may have been a factor. She was very encouraging and had years of good results, but she was very honest. It could be a lengthy process and very expensive, and it could require more than one try. She gave us brochures, DVDs, websites, and blogs from patients who had gone through the same procedure. She wanted us to research and learn as much as we could before we made any kind of final decision. We left with our heads spinning. David felt like a failure and that he had let me down. We stayed up very late, talking and comforting each other. We researched everything we could find on IVF and came to the decision that we would do it. We both felt that we would have regrets if we did not try. I always felt that I could live with my mistakes, but I didn't want to live with regrets. I scheduled the next appointment with Dr. Patel and in two weeks we would sign the consent and start the program.

With all the negatives I had been dealing with, the next week brought some justice and laughter at work. At this time there had been no "Me Too" movement. Inappropriate behavior by surgeons and other physicians was still tolerated by the administration. Surgeons had always been captain of the ship and everyone else just had to put up with their boorish behavior. A pat here, a rub there and sexual jokes and innuendo were all commonplace. The female nurses just learned to avoid it as much as possible and try to get out of the way. Dr. Mason was a neurosurgeon and the king of sexual harassment. He was an excellent surgeon whose patients adored him. However, he was a pig of a man. He would come up behind the nurses as they were scrubbing at the sink and bring his hands around and rub their breasts. Or he would pat their behind or rub against them. He knew they couldn't do much because if they slapped him away, they would have to start to scrub all over again. He used any excuse to cop a feel and he was not selective- old, young, fat, skinny. If you were a woman, you got unwanted attention. There were other surgeons who had this behavior, but on a smaller scale. He was the worst and it had gone on for years. He felt he was lovable and he didn't mean anything negative by his actions. We all warned one another when he came into the OR. If we saw him in the hall, someone would call out "Mason's here" and the nurses went into avoidance mode. This particular day we were having going away treats for one of the nurses and had donuts and snacks set up in the nurse's lounge. There was a doctor's lounge, but everyone always congregated in the nurse's lounge to chat and catch up on the latest gossip. The coffee urn was set up just outside the room on a cart. As it sometimes happens, there was a lull between cases as rooms were being cleaned and changing over. There happened to be a lot of staff in the lounge due to the food. Dr. Mason came in to join the group and was getting a cup of coffee. He had a cup in one hand and the pot in the other. Denise Wells, one of the CRNAs, came up behind him as he was getting his coffee. She reached around his front very slowly and carefully grabbed him right by the balls and said, "Well hello, Dr. Mason, how are you and the boys today?" He was bumbling and stumbling with his face red as a beet. He had no idea what to do and was completely unnerved. The room went crazy. Everyone stood and gave Denise a standing ovation with loud cheering. Dr. Mason could not find words. He put his coffee down and left for the doctor's lounge. Denise was a staff CRNA who had worked there for over 15 years. She was well endowed and had had her share of his antics. We all really laughed and we noticed some of the other doctors taking note. He did not bother Denise again and he toned down his actions with the rest of the staff. Some of the other nurses took strength from her stand and spoke out against this behavior. The situation definitely improved for all of us and Denise became our hero.

Chapter 9

It was spring in Florida, which meant beautiful weather most of the time. We had an appointment the next week to start our IVF. I was scheduled off on Friday and David and I planned a three-day weekend. We decided to go to the beach in Melbourne. Brevard County has beautiful beaches and they were never as crowded as some of the others. David had a friend who lived there and we planned to have dinner with him and his wife on Saturday. Thursday was a foul weather day with bands of severe rain and storms. The sun did not shine the whole day, which is unusual. It was cool, stormy, and raining when I left work. David knew he would be late getting home. He had to go to Daytona Beach to meet with a colleague who was putting together a very complex business insurance package for a client. He planned to bring dinner home. As I drove home the rain had turned into a torrential downpour. I was glad I lived close to the hospital. I checked the weather for the weekend and it was supposed to clear tomorrow and be sunny, so I was happy. Around six o'clock I tried calling David to see when he would be home, but there was no answer. I left a voicemail and sent a text. The rain had let up a bit, but traffic was snarled everywhere. At seven o'clock I called again, but still no answer. Now I was getting worried. David was very good about staying in touch.

I watched the local news and the roads were a mess. At 7:45. I decided that I would run out and get something for dinner. I texted him again and told him to just come home and I would have dinner waiting. The doorbell rang just as I was getting ready to leave. When I opened the door, my heart skipped and I knew immediately. There were two police officers standing there and their faces said it all. I had seen that look many times at the hospital when there was bad news to deliver. I could barely speak. "It's David, isn't it?" I asked. The police don't come for any other reason. They both sadly nodded. "There was an accident on I-4. David stopped to help a woman whose car had broken down. Another driver did not see him in the pouring rain and he was hit by the side of the road. He was killed instantly. We are so sorry. May we call someone for you?" With those few words my husband, my best friend, my lover, my soulmate was gone. Nothing would ever be the same in my life.

I sat in stunned silence while the officers called Teri for me. I know she came immediately and was with me off and on for several days. I really don't remember much about the next two weeks. I called our immediate family, but I don't remember the heartbreaking conversations. Teri called friends and acquaintances. I must have given her names and phone numbers because soon the house was full of people. My brother-in-law went with me to the morgue to identify him and then to help with the funeral arrangements. None of it seemed real. I kept waiting for him to come home and take charge. Even now, those weeks are just a haze. What is crystal clear in my mind is him saying goodbye that Thursday morning when I left for work. That was the last time I ever saw him. Family and friends filled the house for over a week and started drifting home after the funeral. I did not leave the house for 3 weeks, and what I did is shrouded in fog. I just existed.

The hospital was very supportive. They told me to take whatever time off I needed. I wasn't sure I even wanted to go back. Everything about the routine was a reminder of what was no more and I didn't think I could bear it. David had been an excellent planner and very knowledgeable about insurance, so money was not an issue for me. I didn't even need to work if I chose not to. I knew I had to do something, but right now I did not want to leave the house. Teri was a wonderful friend. She shopped for me and came by as often as she could. After it had been six weeks, she started pushing me a little harder to get out. Mitch had been great too. He was close by that first terrible week and had continued to come by often after the family left. It had been almost 2 months now and I was admitting to myself that I couldn't just sit here.

I could hear David admonishing me and telling me to get moving. I was looking on the internet for volunteer opportunities when the doorbell rang. Every time it rang, I could still picture those two police officers ending my life as I knew it. It was Mitch and he brought chili dogs, one of my favorites. "Randy is back," he said. I had not really thought about Randy. I really hadn't thought about anyone. "Wait," I said, "shouldn't he have been back a while ago?" "You're right", Mitch said. "When he was due to be released, he felt he just needed more time. He called me and asked if I thought he could be away another two or three weeks. I met with Pam and we had to do some juggling. She called him and got a few answers she needed regarding the office construction, but we both thought that if he felt he needed the time, he should take it."

Randy was stunned to hear about David, Mitch said. "He would really like to see you. Will you come to dinner with him and me tomorrow night?" I didn't really feel like going anywhere, but I knew I should get out, so I agreed to go. Mitch was pleased that I had accepted and said he would pick me up. It would be a low-key dinner he assured me. I was ambivalent all day. It felt disloyal to David to go on with my life. He was just doing a kindness for someone and his life was over. I know everyone says that life goes on, but only someone who has experienced such a loss can understand these feelings.

Mitch picked me up and we went to a very nice restaurant. I was glad to see it was a small, quiet place. We had just ordered a drink when Randy arrived. We hugged and both cried. He told me how sorry he was about everything. He had liked David very much. He was open about his rehab and how he had let his life get out of control. He and his wife were living separately but had decided to wait for a divorce decision. He was very anxious to move ahead with the new facility. As expected, he found some things that didn't meet his approval, but he was working it out with the contractor. He had high praise for both Pam and Mitch and admitted that he could have never gotten through this without them. He asked if I would come by and talk to him at the new office. He had a proposal that he thought I would be interested in. I knew I would have to drag myself to do it, but I agreed.

Chapter 10

A few days later I decided that I had to do something. Moping would not change anything, and I needed to find a new direction. It was a beautiful bright day and I decided to see Randy. I called Pam and she said it was a good time. He had patients coming at two o'clock, but was there now catching up on paperwork. I picked up lunch for the three of us and decided to hear him out. They were both glad to see me and we drove over for a tour of the new facility. I was surprised at the progress that had been made. It was really state-of-the-art and would be fully accredited. That meant licensing from the state and certification from the American Board of Plastic Surgery. I remembered that years ago state certification wasn't necessary for procedures being done in offices. There had been a number of tragic deaths occurring in dental and physician offices around the state. A south Florida newspaper had done a shocking expose' on the situation. Anesthesia and sedation were being done by unqualified people and some doctors working without vital emergency equipment. It was unbelievable that some medical professionals were so lax. The publicity from the newspaper brought a full investigation and a new set of rules that would apply to every physician in the state who does surgery outside of the hospital. The rules were stringent and necessary to protect the public. He offered me a job setting up protocols and safety standards and seeing it all through to full credentialing.

I knew it was a very involved process and it would take a lot of work to do a thorough job. Pam said a couple of credentialing companies had contacted her, but Randy didn't want that. He wanted a professional he knew with surgical experience to look at their facility in depth. "After we get credentialed", he said, "I would like you to be the anesthesia provider for the facility". He told me to think about it and we would discuss salary and benefits later. I took another walk around and this time I looked at everything differently. I asked if I could have a set of plans to study. He was pleased and knew that I was interested. I was sure he was going to be successful and the challenge might be what I needed. I took the plans home and really studied them. I know about patient flow and safety, and I could get the rules for accreditation. I decided to visit a couple of other surgeons that had similar facilities. There was an orthopedic surgeon I knew from the hospital who had built a beautiful facility. I called and asked if he would allow me to visit on a surgery day to observe his routine. He agreed and I made an appointment. The one thing I didn't know about was salary or benefits in this employment structure. Working in an anesthesia group was easy. We were all paid and treated the same, but I was clueless about this type of working arrangement. It is always easier to do something correctly from the beginning than try to change it later. I started to get excited. This was interesting and different and I dove right in over the next few days. I was soon drowning in rules, regulations and paperwork. I called Randy and accepted the position. He was pleased and invited me to dinner to celebrate. We went to one of the nicest hotel restaurants at Disney with Pam and her husband, Tom, joining us. I told them I wanted to consult with both a lawyer and an accountant to see if I could get some employment advice. I remember David saying that a lot of people don't research contracts or agreements until there's a problem, and then it's often too late. Randy suggested that he pay me a flat fee for all the credentialing and we would work out a fee schedule for future anesthesia. He seemed both fair and agreeable, which made me feel better about my decision. Over the next couple of weeks, I met with both the lawyer and the accountant that David had used. I would form my own company and that would allow me to work for other physicians too. The lawyer handled the company set up and the accountant helped me come up with a method of payment. Now I focused on the patients. I got a copy of the suggested protocols from the AANA. Protocols are a written list of exactly what will be the role of each person in the facility. It defines how care will be rendered pre-op, intra-op and postoperatively. It is specific for each facility. Randy and I would both sign the protocols and submit them to the state. They would be renewed and updated annually. I spent a lot of time studying the patient flow, and in a couple of weeks the plan was really coming together. I saw Mitch and showed him my work. I knew he was planning to do surgery there too, so I wanted his input. He was impressed and enthused with the progress. Initial credentialing had been filed, but we needed an inspection that would be done after all construction and furnishing were complete. It was getting very close to being done. Pam was excited that Teri had come in and was seriously considering the job as nurse supervisor. I did not try to influence her in any way and felt she needed to make up her own mind. I told Randy I was going to take a couple of weeks off to go north. I needed to be near David's and my family. This project had taken my thoughts away from him. He knew nothing about this and it left me feeling a little out of sorts. My life was starting to separate from him. When you lose someone, there is a feeling that you are abandoning them. The adjustment is difficult, but you have to do it. I know people who have gotten stuck in the past and been unable to find happiness in life. Visiting family can sometimes give you the root support you need at the time. By the time I got back, the building should be done and we could get ready for final inspection. They had finally met with Charity Levele, the marketing director, and a planning meeting was set up. I was glad I would be back so I could participate. I was organizing the anesthesia equipment and checking the narcotic storage when I heard the new sign had arrived. We ran out to take a look and there it was on the front of the building. "Never Settle for Mediocrity", Randall Tanner MD, FACS, Plastic and Cosmetic Surgery". Pam and I did a little congratulatory dance. I finished my work, hugged her goodbye and left to get ready for my trip.

Chapter 11

My family visit was bittersweet with more tears than laughter, but I had to accept the new reality. My family was wonderful. My cousin organized a reunion that brought in cousins, aunts, uncles, former neighbors, and coworkers. I got a much-needed lift. David's family was struggling, but very supportive of me. After 2 weeks I was ready to come home and get my mind busy. I had purposely not called or checked on anything with the new surgery center. I needed to focus on getting my life back to some kind of new normal. On the flight home I thought about the new practice and how this could be a really exciting and fun position. It is so true that ignorance is bliss.

I was up early the next day, went to the grocery store first and headed to the clinic. I was surprised at the progress. It was down to the pretty work and it looked beautiful. There was a full wall waterfall in the waiting room decorated in blue, beige, and peach and it was very Florida. I was pleased with the surgery area. There were boxes and equipment around, but it was a real surgical suite. "Well, what do you think?" asked a cheerful Randy. "Wow is all

I can say," I said as I gave him a hello hug. He walked me around pointing out the highlights. The OR was set up the same as the hospital with new high-end monitoring equipment. I was impressed and pleased that this was my new work environment. Mitch stopped by to check progress and we walked him through. We had him play patient and lie on the OR table. I hooked up the monitors and tried all the table positions. We were anxious to start seeing patients, but we had to get the final inspection. It was scheduled for 2 weeks away. Teri had accepted the position as nurse supervisor just after I left and had been coming in while I was away. Randy had hired Becky Bronson as his scrub tech and he was very pleased. She was great at her job and both Randy and Mitch requested her a lot at the hospital. She had 10 years of experience and was ready to get rid of the night and weekend call. She had a tough life with an ill mom and an ex-husband who couldn't keep a job. Randy recognized the importance of a committed scrub tech and made her a very good offer. He was nervous about the inspection, but ready to go full steam once we were approved. He was excited about the marketing team coming in soon for the planning session. My mind was spinning with all the things I needed to do. Mitch and I walked out together and he seemed quiet. "Are you ok, Mitch?" I asked. He stopped and looked at me. "He's really going fast. There is a lot of stress in a project this size. Not to mention the financial aspect. My small practice is a lot of headaches and it is nothing like this. I hope he can deal with all of it ok." I agreed with him, but pointed out that he had been driven since he came to town and seemed to thrive at this pace. Mitch said Randy was always good, if he was in control. We hugged goodbye and I went to meet Teri. She was stressing about the inspection and we were going to go brainstorm a few last-minute issues.

Becky was concerned that we had not hired anyone for terminal cleaning. That is a term for specialized cleaning done in the OR at the end of the day. There is a written protocol that requires every surface to be cleaned in a specific way. A general cleaning and mopping are done between cases, but terminal is much more intense and often done by people with special training. Becky said "I think you know Wesley Ford from the hospital. He is in charge of all the OR cleaning services. I heard that he does some outside work after hours and I ran it by him. He does some other physician facilities and he's interested. You want me to set up a meeting for you?" Teri jumped at that.

Inspection day came and we were ready. There is always some last-minute problem that comes up and we had one the day before. One of the narcotic lock box keys was missing. There were 3 originally. I had one, Pam had one in the safe but Teri's was gone. She was sure where she left it, but it was not there. These keys cannot be duplicated. You must get a new one from the vendor where you purchased the narcotic box. Fortunately, our vendor was still open and we got it overnighted. Randy was a bundle of nerves, pacing around and questioning everyone. The inspection was scheduled for 10:00 a.m. and Charity Levele and her team were coming at 4:00 p.m. to present the marketing plan. It was going to be a big day.

By 7:30 am we were back running around checking and rechecking everything. At 10 a.m. a pleasant doctor and nurse from the state Board arrived and began examining every nook and cranny. Randy offered to send out for lunch, but they declined. Around noon they sat down with the protocols and policy and procedure manuals. They asked questions of all of us while they took photos and made copies. It was nearly 3:00 when they finished. They were complimentary to Randy and said that he would know if the center was approved in 2 to 3 weeks. We received a temporary permit, so we could begin seeing patients. When they left, we gave a collective sigh of relief. It was over and we had done our best. Pam had ordered lunch when she saw we were finishing and we dug in before the arrival of the marketing group.

Promptly at 4:00 the marketing team arrived. Charity Levele was an attractive, well- dressed woman with a warm smile and a no-nonsense demeanor. She introduced her associates, who were already looking over the facility. There was a photographer and graphic designer and an administrative assistant. Charity joked that she was their gofer, but there was no question as to who was the boss. She said the first marketing opportunity begins when your phone rings or you receive an email asking for information. The marketing plan would formulate instructions on responses to potential patients. Patient targeting would come from multiple sources, including print, TV, radio, lectures and the internet. The photos of the facility would attest to its comfort and safety and they would also be used in brochures or any print advertising. She mentioned that she had seen the basic website that Randy had been using, but felt it was not adequate. She wanted a new more professional website that was easier to navigate. This was the mid 2000's and social media was not the same as today. She mentioned targeting specific groups for presentation and information. Women were the primary users of cosmetic surgery and there were many clubs and groups that provided lectures to their members. There was also the possibility of having informational seminars here at the facility. She also knew a man who owned several gentlemen's clubs and was interested in meeting a surgeon. Some of the dancers had surgery and were not happy with the results, so he was looking for a new referral doctor. Pam said they had many happy patients who would write a testimonial regarding their experience and Teri mentioned community health care events. Also, there were a couple of large women-centered events held annually. Ideas were really flowing when Charity said she wanted to introduce the big decision. We all looked at each other wondering what she meant. "A billboard," she said. Randy mulled it a bit and said there are a few billboards used by professionals, but he wondered how it would be received. "They are everywhere in south Florida", she said. "And there are a couple in north Orlando for eye clinics. You would be one of the first plastic surgeons, but I bet you won't be the last. A photo of you with clinical descriptions and your practice statement, "Never Settle for Mediocrity". Randy liked it. The conversation started winding down and the assistant surprised us. "May I use your copy machine?" she asked Pam. They went to the front office and returned with a printed list of all the suggestions that we discussed. "Feel free to add or delete whatever ideas you like or dislike", Charity said in summary. We loved how organized the presentation had been. She summed it up. "We will put all of this into a working plan with specifics. There will be recommendations for what we suggest you do first. Also, I would like to meet once a month for the first 3 months, then as needed. Please review everything when you receive the proposal and if you decide to go with it,

I will return with the contracts". They gathered their belongings, thanked everyone, and left. We sat there looking at one another. "Wow," I said. "That is a high-energy group". Pam was very enthused. "I think they spell success," she said. "I think they spell money", Randy laughed. "But they are probably well worth it. I know we all feel brain-dead about now, but we are seeing our first patients on Monday." Pam had scheduled the first day to allow extra time and there were 8 consults. That would be a good day. Just as we were leaving, Mitch stopped by to take Randy to dinner to celebrate the day.

Chapter 12

I did not have anything at the center Monday, but I planned to stop by around 4:00. Becky had made arrangements for Wes Ford to stop by and discuss the terminal cleaning. I planned to take care of all of my own equipment. I had never been comfortable with other people handling any of it. I was interested in his general cleaning regime. He was a great guy who had started out in the hospital stockroom receiving area when he was 18. Hard work had paid off and he went next to janitorial, then central supply, and then OR cleaning. Now 10 years later he was the supervisor of all procedural and terminal cleaning in the hospital. He had taken classes in microbiology, blood-borne pathogens, and hazardous materials. He took his job very seriously. Since a number of physicians had outside facilities, he had developed a side business providing cleaning services to them. Everything I had heard was very positive, so I was hoping he would join our team. I was also anxious to hear how the first day of consults went.

I got there early and Pam was flying high. All the patients had come in and were very complimentary to the facility. Three patients had scheduled surgery. Two were new and one was a repeat patient, who I remembered. I knew Carrie from the hospital outpatient department where she had surgery before. She was an interesting woman. She had lived in Alaska, where residents are given an annual share of profits from the trans-Alaska pipeline. She had lived there with her husband for years and said it was brutal sometimes. When she divorced, it was part of the agreement that her ex would give her the payment he received from the state. He did and she used that money for cosmetic surgery every year. She had been coming to Randy since he came to Orlando. She said she believed some of the older movie stars had the right idea. They had small nips and tucks done more frequently, rather than big changes all at once. She was pleasant and fun and I looked forward to seeing her. Pam said a couple of the others were still pending. It sounded like a very good first day. Randy gave a quick hello and ran out the door. He had an ER call to see a severe facial dog bite.

Wes arrived at 4:00 and he had a written protocol outlining exactly how he would clean every surface. We were impressed. Our plan was to have surgery on Monday, Tuesday, and Thursday, but we were keeping an open mind on everything and willing to change if we saw a better way. Wes said he would be the main person doing the cleaning, but he would not always be available. He had been training Zach Houston, one of his employees in his side business. He said Zach was currently working at the hospital and he had known him a long time. He would bring him in and give him specific training for us. It sounded good and Pam told Wes we would get Randy's final approval and let him know.

I suggested we go for an early dinner. I wanted to talk about the grand opening gala that Randy was planning. Pam asked if she could bring her husband, Tom, and Teri and I said absolutely. He was fun and always had ideas that we would have never considered. Becky said her mom was not doing well and she needed to get home, but she would help in any way she could.

We loved a popular taco place that had tasty margaritas and tableside guacamole. Tom talked us out of it and suggested a smaller quieter place down the road. "I love the place, but we can't hear one another. Let's go where we can brainstorm a bit." He was right and that's what we did.

Randy was determined to make the grand opening a real blowout, and he wanted to showcase his beautiful facility. There was still work to be done in the spa area and he wanted that open before the gala. Pam was acquainted with Nancy McAllan, who had worked at a high-end spa for years. She was a medical aesthetician and was in high demand. Randy met her and offered her the manager position. She was very enthusiastic and had been coming in frequently following the spa progress. She had started interviewing for employees and had written a protocol for each of the services that would be provided.

We also hired a Recovery room nurse, Claudia Kent. Teri knew her from the hospital and she would also do the overnight patients.

The next month was very busy. We had 7 patients on the surgery schedule for the next week, but we had not received the state certification yet. We had a temporary permit, but we were not doing surgery. Pam was dreading having to reschedule people. She thought it would make us look disorganized. It was Friday and Teri had asked me to come in because she was going to reorganize some storage and she wanted me to be aware of it. We heard a big Yay from the front and Pam came back waving the certificate from the state. We were approved and could commence doing surgery. Now that we were state-approved, we could apply to be credentialed by the American Board of Plastic Surgery. Randy was doing hospital surgery today, but we knew he would be calling as soon as he was done. Pam decided she would call each patient, confirm the times, and go over instructions again. I reviewed the charts and made sure no one had medical issues that needed to be addressed. We had breast augmentations, breast lifts and one tummy tuck scheduled. The tummy tuck was my concern. Randy had decided that face lift and tummy tuck patients would stay overnight at the facility. These were long cases and he wanted the patients to be observed and cared for by a nurse.

The Levele team came back with an ambitious marketing plan. Randy agreed to go with the billboard and they scheduled a photo shoot.

Charity had arranged a lunch with Randy and Mark Foley, who owned 3 topless clubs in the Orlando area and 2 in Tampa. She also had arranged a meeting at 3 local TV stations and one radio station. Medical news was always of interest and she wanted his name to become familiar to the media. She said she had contacted a few local groups, including a professional business women's association, a teacher's organization, a retired sorority and a retired women's philanthropy group. All were interested in having Randy speak. She left Pam's contact information for scheduling purposes. Randy was fired up. He loved the excitement and the potential.

The first few weeks were exciting and our cases were going well. Patients were pleased with their surgical outcomes and we were starting to see word of mouth new patients. Cosmetic surgery patients were proving very interesting. There are many reasons people look at cosmetic surgery. Sometimes it is something they have had all their life, but never liked. Family and friends pooh-pooh it, but you see it every time you look in the mirror. It can be a mole, a scar, small or large breasts, or your nose. Now that you are an adult, you can choose to change it, and many people do. Breast augmentation is the most common procedure done in the U.S. It is not just done for those seeking fame. I talk to all of my patients about their hopes, motivations, and reasons, which are varied. There are some who do it for business reasons. Modeling, topless dancing, movies (porno and traditional), or any type of acting performance. At this time transgender augmentations were done, but not frequently. The biggest reason is the average woman just wants to look better, feel more confident and increase her self-esteem. Many women lose breast volume after pregnancy and breastfeeding and they just want to look like they did before. There are some women who get surgery as part of a divorce settlement. They are sometimes called mommy makeovers. This can include a tummy tuck and/or a breast lift. I found the topless dancers to be a very interesting group of women. Many people assume that these women just want attention, aren't smart enough to do anything else or are supporting a drug habit. This may be true for some, but not all of the women I met. Many of them were paying for college, so they wouldn't have student debt. One was paying for her husband's medical school. A couple were supporting aged parents. I learned that Mark Foley was like many club owners. He owned multiple locations and would rotate the girls performing, so the clientele wouldn't get tired of them. Some of the girls were coming out of rehab or abusive situations and were trying to rebuild their lives. Some were still living in these situations, but they didn't tend to last long. They made a lot of money, so it was a chance and not everyone made it. I remember one girl who worked for a lobbyist in New Jersey. She had 2 sisters dancing in Orlando and had come to visit. They went to the beach, shopping and theme parks. The lobbyist called constantly hounding the girl with work issues. Her sisters danced 4 nights for 6 hours. They compared paychecks. She went back to New Jersey to get her clothes and resign. Her goal was dancing, banking money, and then an advanced degree.

There was one person who stood out to me when we had been working for a few months. He was a very flamboyant larger-than-life kind of guy named Lonnie Gretsky, who came in with his girlfriend. He had tried to dictate the size and shape her implants would be and she didn't get a word in. Randy shut him right down. He strongly felt that this was the woman's decision and if the man couldn't keep quiet, he would have to leave the room. Lonnie was very apologetic and behaved, but I knew his wishes would be met by his girlfriend. He arrived with her on the day of surgery and brought in a big box of donuts for the staff. He kept everyone entertained right up until discharge. We meet him again.

The spa was finally open and it was beautiful. There were the usual spa services such as facials, peels, skincare advice, massages, products, Botox, fillers, and little extras. Anyone having facial surgery received a complimentary shampoo after surgery. Many times, you couldn't shower immediately after surgery and the patients loved getting their hair clean. All face lift patients received a skin care and makeup consult post-surgery. Nancy had good contacts among aestheticians and she had hired a great staff. Pam, Becky, Teri, Claudia and I loved it. We could get whatever we wanted and just tip the staff for their time. Randy said we deserved it and we agreed.

Chapter 13

Time was approaching for the grand opening gala. The guest list was growing. We decided to have the facility open and have a large tent with food and a full bar outside. Pam made a great invitation and asked all of us to think about who we should invite. Charity also provided a list of must-invites. Randy had met many people in his speaking engagements and clubs that he had joined. His list included medical reporters from the newspaper and TV channels, other local plastic surgeons, current patients, local high visibility attorneys, other physicians on local hospital medical boards, our local congressmen (both political parties), medical lobbyists, and 2 of Randy's friends that were serving on the state board of medicine. He said he knew a lot of invitees would not come, but thought it would be good that all of them knew he was up and running. Pam was hoping people would RSVP, but nowadays not everyone did. She was worried about running out of food or drinks. Her husband, Tom, suggested getting extra alcohol and a stash of food that could be heated if needed and frozen if we didn't use it. He also wanted to invite a friend that he golfed with, Buddy Baker. He was a very popular morning radio show talk jock. Tom had given him some very good financial advice and they had become friends. Buddy had no political affiliations and would trash anyone. He had the coveted 6 a.m. to 9 a.m. travel time slot and worked with a very upbeat and fun staff. Randy had not met him and thought it was a great idea to invite him. It was scheduled for May, which is usually really nice Florida weather.

The billboard went up on a busy area along I-4. His photo had captured the perfect pose. Randy was wearing his white coat with a muted operating room background. His handsome face had a smile, but also a serious and concerned look. His message was Never Settle for Mediocrity. Come to his cosmetic center for the best surgery experience and result. It created quite a buzz. He got criticism from other plastic surgeons that he was unprofessional. He also got praise for how forward-thinking he was. He felt it was a sign of the times. Dental clinics, attorneys, and eye surgeons all used billboards, so why not him? Meanwhile, his phone was ringing off the hook. Pam was scheduling consults weeks out.

In just a few months we were doing 10-15 cases a week. I was pleased that so far, we had only minor problems and I enjoyed the patients. Randy didn't see consults on surgery days, but one patient traveled and had a very demanding schedule. She was a professional women's MMA fighter and prior to that had been a professional wrestler. She came in at the end of our surgery day. Randy called me into his office and introduced me to her. I was surprised to see that she was a mature woman, not what you would think with this type of sport, but she was in amazing shape. Randy told me she wanted an extended tummy tuck with a lower body lift, but he was concerned about the scar because of her costumes. She wanted a woman's opinion. She flung off her clothes and said to me "What do you think?" I thought, I wish I looked that good. It wouldn't be a big tummy tuck, but she had children and wanted the abdominal muscle tightened. I did understand Randy's concern. In order to do the lower body lift to tighten around to the hip and upper thigh area, the tummy tuck scar would have to be extended around to the back. He warned it could possibly be seen in her costumes. She said she knew she only had a few years left in the field and she needed to look really competitive. I handed Randy a Sharpie and he drew the scar location and let her see it. "That is a big scar," she said. He nodded. "That's why I wanted you to see it. You have an olive complexion and the scar may not heal really flat. It could be red for a long time too. You have to be sure you can live with that". I asked if there was some type of makeup or cover-up she could use. Suddenly she smiled and said "What about a tattoo? I could get something to go all around my waist and onto my back." Randy thought and said "That would probably work. But you can't get anything like that done until you are completely healed." She jumped up and gave both of us a hug. "I'm going to get a coiled hissing snake wrapping around with rattles on the tail. I'll use emeralds for eyes and a ruby in my new belly button for the tongue. I love it. I'm off for a couple of months this summer. How do I get on the schedule?" And that is exactly what she did.

The grand opening was a huge success. We waited until everything was open and running smoothly. We had been open over 6 months. It was a beautiful Friday evening. The staff did guest tours and answered lots of questions. Randy brought his wife and children. I had not met her before. She was a lovely quiet woman, who kept the children close to her. Mitch was there helping Randy give special attention and tours to the VIPs. The tent and the office were full. Randy had gotten a radio DJ he knew to provide pleasant background music. Pam said many people there had not sent an RSVP and the caterer was concerned they were getting low on food. She was relieved when she saw Tom's reserve of appetizers in the freezer. Pam lost count and guessed there were over 200 people coming and going. Randy asked me to take 2 of his friends on a tour of the surgery and recovery rooms. He wanted me to explain our patient flow and answer any questions. They were his good friends and were both on the state board of medicine. They were very interested and impressed with the facility. I noticed Zach Houston, Wes Ford's cleaning employee. He seemed really drunk and was annoying Claudia. I asked if he was bothering her. "I think he is out of it," she said. "He was being inappropriate and I told him to go sit in the kitchen." I went looking for him. I was going to tell him to leave, but I couldn't find him. Teri told me she had seen him being an ass. She followed him into the kitchen and told him to leave. We were definitely going to speak to Wes about him. The DJ ended at 8:30 and the caterer was cleaning up. By 9:00 everyone was gone. Randy had left with his friends from the board, Mitch and 2 lobbyists whom I had not met. The staff crashed in the waiting room. Teri looked around and said, "Do we have to clean up tonight?" Pam smiled. "Thank Tom. He scheduled a cleaning crew in tomorrow morning. He offered to come over and supervise the job, so we don't have to worry about it. Let's just split up any food that won't keep". We had all enjoyed it, but were glad it was over.

Chapter 14

Business was booming. Randy was easily working 60–70-hour weeks, sometimes more. He still took ER plastic surgery call and we were trying to convince him to trade his days away. Mitch said he would be glad to take it because most of his practice was non-cosmetic. We convinced him to take a week off. He took his children north to visit his family and we all enjoyed a week off too. Teri met with Wes and told him how inappropriate Zach had been at the opening. He said he would talk to him, but defended him. He said they had been friends since elementary school and Zach had a bad home life. Teri said that a lot of people had a tough home life and that was no excuse. She said she was going to keep an eye on him and she meant it.

On our first surgery day back to work, Randy called all of us into his office. "We have a bit of a situation and I just want to be sure everyone is tuned into patient confidentiality. Our previous friend, Lonnie Gretsky, who came in with a girlfriend a while back, is coming back with another patient. This time it is his wife. We must be sure that no one recognizes him or in any way lets on that we know him. She is on the schedule this week, so please be very careful. This is a personal matter and we must protect everyone's privacy." Teri asked if we thought he would bring donuts and everyone laughed.

The day turned into an interesting one for me. One of my patients, Starr, was a gorgeous 30-year-old blond with a great figure having a liposuction. As usual, I asked her about her motivation for surgery. She took a flyer out of her purse and said "This is the reason". There she was in full color dressed in black leather as a dominatrix. She looked both frightening and alluring. She nodded at the flyer and said "This was a couple of years ago. I have added a bit of flab and I have to get back down to this look". "Is this a costume or is this your work?" I asked. She proceeded to tell me that a little over 10 years ago her husband moved her and 2 toddlers to Florida and after a couple of months had abandoned them. She had come from a poor and dysfunctional family and had no one who could help her. They were living in a small motel that catered to transient workers. The woman who owned the motel felt sorry for her and let her clean and work in the motel to give her a place to live.

One day the woman's daughter, Alynn, came to see her mother. She was older than Starr, but very beautiful and drove a Porsche. She was interested in Starr and knew her story. She offered to take her for a makeover while her mom watched the children. Starr jumped at it. She had done nothing but worry since her husband had left. She had a facial, highlights in her hair and makeup applied. She had felt so haggard that she had forgotten how good she could look. Driving back to the motel, Alynn asked if Starr would like to make some money. "I'm not a prostitute, Alynn. I just couldn't do that. I don't judge anyone else, but I can't do it." She assured Starr that she wasn't talking about prostitution. "Do you know", she said "that men or women pay for sexual gratification in many ways that do not involve sexual contact? Have you ever heard of a foot fetish? I live in Tampa and there is a retired judge who has seen me twice a month for several years. I wear certain kinds of shoes and foot jewelry and he loves my feet. We have a special dialogue that he likes and I stay with him for an hour and a half with no sex. I have other clients that have unusual needs. They all pay extremely well. You are lovely and kind. I think you could take good care of your children with a bit of training and no sex. What do you think?" When they pulled into the gloomy motel and her children ran to meet her, she knew she had to try anything that would get them into a better life style. Eventually she learned the ropes and developed her own clientele in Orlando. She occasionally went back to Tampa for an old client, but was as busy as she needed to be here. "I'm very grateful to Alynn. I have a beautiful home, my kids are in private school and I divorced that bum. The dominatrix role is for those clients who request it, but I play whatever role they need. You would be shocked if you saw my client list" she told me. I congratulated her on turning her life around and we moved on to perfecting her lovely figure.

A couple of days later, as I was setting up my anesthesia case, I heard this loud familiar voice. It was Lonnie with his wife. Of course all of us called him Mr. Gretsky. "Call me Lonnie. I have donuts for everyone" he said. We were all very careful about what we said. After the surgery, I came out to tell him his wife had done very well and I quietly said. "Lonnie, if you come again, please bring jelly-filled.

They are my favorite". He laughed and thanked everyone for being a good sport.

Pam told the staff at the end of the week that Randy had made an agreement with Mark Foley to give the girls from his clubs special prices. Another club owner in Tampa was also going to send us patients. He was using a nearby plastic surgeon, but many of the girls were not happy with their surgery. She said we would probably be seeing more dancers. We had been working now for almost 10 months and had found that the majority of the patients were great, but there were a few that were not compliant with instructions. We had a couple of infections and one girl had broken open her skin closure from aggressive sex the day after surgery. Teri really went over instructions and started to get a feel for anyone who didn't treat surgery seriously.

There was one patient who was scheduled for breast augmentation at 1:00 and came in with her boyfriend and his male friend. Pam alerted me as soon as she noticed her carrying a coffee cup. When I finished my case, I went out to the waiting area, greeted them and asked if she had been drinking coffee. She angrily resented my asking. "Of course, not" she barked. I noticed the friend looked at her strangely. "It is vital that you not have anything to eat or drink", I told her. "You were carrying a coffee cup when you came in. It is very serious. You could aspirate fluid into your lungs and die." She was very defensive. "Do you think I'm stupid? I said I didn't have anything to eat or drink, so that's it. You're running late, so why don't you get things organized instead of wasting time harassing me?" I didn't believe her. She was overreacting and she had a bad attitude. I went in and told Randy and expressed my feelings. He called them into his office with me. He addressed the coffee issue and she had the same bad attitude with him. Randy said it was my call. If I didn't want to do the anesthesia, we would cancel the surgery. She became belligerent and demanded her money back. He said it was up to her. We were only concerned with her safety. The male friend stood up and said she was lying. She not only had coffee, but had eaten a breakfast sandwich. He said he wasn't going to sit there and see someone do something stupid and dangerous and he walked out. We just looked at her and she started crying. I left the room and a little later I saw them talking to Pam and rescheduling. The boyfriend said he was sorry and she would be back following instructions. Pam made her wait a month until there was an 8 a.m. appointment available. I am always amazed when patients don't follow instructions. They are there for only one reason and that is to help protect their safety.

Chapter 15

We were heading into the holiday season. The holidays were so busy that we decided to have an early office holiday gathering. Randy took us to a very pricey but wonderful dinner at one of the Disney hotels. Mitch came and told us that he was going to pursue more cosmetic cases and would be using the OR. He had done a few cases and we loved and encouraged him. After dinner, Randy hit us with his latest endeavor. He said that through Mark Foley he had met the publisher of Bad Girls Only magazine. They were doing a feature on a particular girl who was going to have a breast augmentation as part of a feature contest. They were coming to do photos and a video of the procedure. "That magazine is no Playboy," Claudia said. "No one buys it for the commentary." I offered jokingly. Randy was a bit defensive. "Look I know this is a rag magazine, but it's going to get a lot of publicity because of the storyline with the patient. I can't get into it now, but I think there should be privacy and no other patients that day. It should be on a Friday. Pam, I will put you in touch with the scheduling people from the magazine." Mitch laughed and said "Someone has to do it.

Better Randy than me, but he's right. It will get publicity." We were skeptical, but he was the boss.

It was scheduled for a Friday morning a few weeks later. Randy called us into his office. "This is an unusual situation. The magazine is doing a feature to coincide with a contest being promoted on some radio show from Chicago. They are paying for the patient to have a breast augmentation as part of the contest. Pam, who already knew the situation, rolled her eyes. "What is the contest?" I asked. Randy squirmed a bit and said "She is going to attempt to break the record for having sex with the most men in the least amount of time. The article is going to start with her having this surgery to prepare and then follow it through to the actual contest. "There is actually a record for this?" Teri asked. Randy smiled. "I guess so, but we have nothing to do with that part of it. We do regular surgery and treat her like any other patient. Sunny, do you have a problem with the film makers being in the OR?" "I will talk to them before and make sure they know the rules" I said. If these guys were creepy, I would discuss it with Randy again. On the day of surgery, the videographers arrived early for set up and the patient arrived a few minutes later.

The 2 men came in and introduced themselves as Willy and Dennis. They were friendly and pleasant. I told them there were rules that had to be followed and they could not come into the room until the patient was asleep and properly draped. Dennis laughed and said it didn't matter because everyone was going to see her anyway. Willy gave him a glare. I said I didn't care what they thought, but we made the rules here and they could follow them or leave. He was immediately contrite and they both knew we did not take surgery lightly. Teri came over with instructions about where they could stand and what they could not touch. I went to see the patient. She was a beautiful girl 22 years old and looked like a college coed. She was nervous and biting her nails. I spent time chatting and going over her health history, trying to relax her a bit. She was a little weepy. "Do you really want to do this?" I asked. "You can change your mind. Are you sure this is what you want?" She smiled a little and said "Yes, I'm sure. It's a chance for real success in this field. It can lead to porn movies and that can be big money. I really want to do it." But I could see tears running down her cheeks. "You seem to be unhappy and that's why I want to be sure you are not being pressured." She wiped her cheeks and said there was only one thing she was really worried about. I took her hand and said, "Tell me." "I don't want my mother to find out." She said with downcast eyes. I had no answer for her but felt this was the time for sedation.

Once she was under anesthesia and properly draped, I told Teri to let the guys in. Willy did still shots and Dennis did the video. They did a brief interview with Randy about his markings and a description of how the procedure was done. Randy chatted a bit as he worked. I knew nothing about porn or sex contests, so I was curious. Teri wanted to know more too, so she was poking me to ask. "Listen guys, Teri and I don't know how this works. How many men will it take to break the record?" Willy said, "I think it's 125 in 2 ½ hours". Teri and I were wide-eyed. "How can that be? That sounds impossible". The guys laughed. "They have a little help," Dennis said. Willy asked us "Have you ever heard of a fluffer?" We had not. "The men sign up for the contest, sign releases, get tested for STDs, and are taken to a room. There are girls there who prepare the men with stimulation and oral sex to get them really ready. They bring them in one at a time and it's usually just in and out and bring in the next one." Willy laughed. "You two look shocked". I looked at Teri and said "There's a whole other world out there." Willy laughed, "You don't know the half of it." The case finished and she did well. We hired an agency nurse to transport and care for her at a hotel. We never found out if she broke the record or saw the article. At least Randy never admitted to it.

Chapter 16

Charlie Devon was driving down I-4 toward a restaurant he had read about when he saw the billboard. There was Randy staring down encouraging people to come to his plastic surgery center. Never Settle for Mediocrity it said. The rage and anger in him were so consuming that he had to pull off the road. He was shaking and actually felt nauseous. He knew Randy was in Orlando, but he had not planned to see or contact him. Seeing that smug face made him sick. All he could picture was his dad on his deathbed blaming himself. Once he was able to drive, he took the next exit, turned around, and went back to his hotel. Once in his room, he let the tears flow. All these years, all of this time, and no one knew. He took a couple of aspirin and lay down on the bed. The memories filled his brain and he could not stop them.

He and Randy had grown up in a small town in Connecticut. They were inseparable playmates since first grade. Charlie's dad, Ron, owned a construction company, and his mom, Susan, who had always had heart problems, stayed home to look after him and his sister, Laura. Randy was an only child. His father, Frank, was a lawyer and his mother, Cheryl, was a paralegal for his dad's firm. Charlie's family was very religious and the children went to Catholic school. Randy's family was not Catholic, but the school was the best in the area and that was where Randy went. There were quite a few non-Catholic families that sent their children to the private school. The boys were in the same grade, played the same sports, went to the same camps and shared the same interests. The families were in different social circles, but were friendly and shared driving the children to events. Cheryl enjoyed occasionally spending time with Laura because she did not have a daughter. In high school, the boys were very big in sports. Football, basketball and baseball. They convinced Frank to teach them golf and got to be pretty good. In the summers they fished with Ron. Susan's health was fragile and her main interest was helping at the church. She was involved with all of the fundraising projects and helping the few nuns who were left at the school. She was very computer literate. Laura worried about her mother and spent a lot of time with her. Susan was always encouraging her to do more with her friends, but Laura preferred to be home or helping at church. She supported any endeavor that involved Charlie. She loved her brother, but she adored Randy. He was her dream. She had a huge crush on him since she was 11 years old and announced that she would marry Randy when she grew up. She got a lot of teasing, but she didn't care. She wanted to ask Randy to junior prom, but Susan said no. Randy was already in college and he was too old for her at this point in her life. She didn't go to the prom. The boys went to the same state university. Randy was in premed and Charlie was in technology. His mother had exposed him to computers and video games as a youngster. She had taught him coding and computers were his love. They stayed close the first year and by the second year they still saw each other, but started to drift in other directions. Laura graduated from high school and went to the same university. She had also developed a real interest in computers from her mother and graphic design was her goal. Susan's health was failing even more and Laura wanted to delay college a year and be home to help her mother. Susan wouldn't hear of it, so Laura went. She would see Charlie frequently and Randy occasionally. She would still get butterflies and her heart would pound when she saw him. He was so gorgeous. She got good grades and was really looking forward to the summer break. She wanted to help her mom reorganize things at home to make it easier for her to get around. Charlie met her for dinner shortly before his graduation and told her about a big fraternity good-bye party that was coming up in a couple of weeks. He and Randy would be graduating and this would be a gathering of a large group of friends. She was excited because she would be one of just a few freshmen there. Charlie had discouraged her from going to any frat parties. He told her stories about drinks being spiked and other bad behaviors. She had still gone to a few, but was very cautious. They were really fun though, and she was looking forward to the party.

The day of the party Charlie called and sounded terrible. He had laryngitis and a fever. He could barely get out of bed. "I'm sorry, Little Kid", which he often called her. "I can't make it. I'll be lucky to live the night." Laura sighed, disappointed. "You are so dramatic, Charlie. Maybe you will feel better later." "I'm going to the campus clinic and see if I can get some meds. I have a fever of 101. Don't worry. You can go with Randy. He said he would take you." "Do you need me to come and help you?" she asked. "No. I'll be ok. You go and have fun. Randy will look out for you." She felt bad for Charlie but was very excited about going with Randy. This was almost a real date.

She dressed carefully and looked terrific. Her roommate called her a traffic stopper. Randy picked her up at the dorm and he was even more handsome than she remembered. "Wow," he said. "When did you grow up to look like this? I can still see you as this skinny kid. Come on and we will have some fun. I'm really sorry Charlie can't be here. This is our last hurrah and then it will be getting down to real business". The party was being held at a great facility. The father of one of the students had rented it. He was an executive and his company had access to use it for business retreats. The place was packed and liquor was flowing. A few students gave humorous eulogies to the departing students. Randy was popular and a couple were directed to him. Laura remembered the warnings from Charlie about keeping her drink in sight at all times. Randy checked back on her often and he was definitely in the bag. She didn't blame him for partying. He would never see many of these friends again. A girl she knew from one of her classes came by and asked if she wanted a little pick-me-up. She pointed to a group over in one corner and said she could get some coke. Laura thanked her but declined. When she looked over, she saw Randy was in the group and thought maybe she would tell him that she should drive home. She danced and laughed and had a couple more drinks. It was a fun night. She walked to the patio doors and looked out at the lovely spring evening. She felt someone come behind her and whisper how beautiful she looked. It was Randy and he kissed the back of her neck. Her knees felt weak and her heart was pounding. She turned and smiled at him and he kissed her passionately. How many times had she dreamed of this? She had loved him all of her life. She couldn't believe it was real. "Come with me", he said. She couldn't say no. He whispered to her as he led her into one of the bedrooms. She knew where this was heading and that she should stop it. She had always vowed to herself that she would stay a virgin until marriage. Some of her friends made fun of her and called her a prude, but it was important to her. Now here she was giving it away.

She hesitated a bit, but she had always loved him. Randy was a practiced lover and there was no turning back. He said he was surprised that she was a virgin. There aren't very many in college he said. Afterward, he rolled over and fell asleep. She immediately regretted it. I should never have done this, she thought. She wanted to talk to Randy, so she shook him a little. No response. He had passed out. I didn't realize he was so drunk, she thought, and then he had the coke or maybe something else. She started to cry. She would talk to him later. He must care about her after what he had said and his passion. She got dressed and went back to the party. The crowd had thinned out and a few people were dozing on couches and chairs. She noticed some people coming out of the bedrooms. Sex is probably a common thing at these parties. How could I be so naïve? I have failed myself and I'm just a fool she thought. She went back once more and tried to wake Randy, but he was out cold. She found her phone and called a taxi to take her home.

Graduation came for Charlie and Randy. Laura hoped to get a chance to see Randy and talk about what had happened. She had been depressed and angry at herself for not handling the situation. He had been drunk and high, but she had not, so she felt it was mostly her fault. If she knew he cared for her or if they could be in some kind of relationship, she would feel better. She sat through the ceremony with her beaming parents and watched Charlie happily receive his diploma. She saw Randy and his parents and saw that, like Charlie, he was wearing an honors sash. Afterward, they walked outside in the crush of people to look for Charlie. She felt someone take her arm. Randy came to greet them and pulled her aside. "I'm going to steal Laura for a minute. I think Charlie is over near the benches" he said and waved them away. He looked very sheepish and could hardly look at her. "I want to apologize for what happened at the party. I was totally wasted. I had been drinking most of the day and then hit a little heavy stuff. I know I was out of line." Before she could respond he went on. "I don't really remember what happened, but I have flashes of me putting the make on you. I'm really sorry, Laura, I was inappropriate. I should know better. Once I start drinking, I don't know when to stop. I wanted you to know that I was an ass and I'm sorry". She was crushed. "You don't remember anything?" "Not much. I remember you were very beautiful and I kissed you a few times. I have flashes of us making out pretty heavy. I hope I wasn't aggressive. Good luck this next school year. I am going to hunt up Charlie now. Again, I'm sorry, Laura. You are a wonderful person and will be very successful in life. Remember, never settle for mediocrity". And he was gone.

Dad invited a group of friends to dinner at a really nice restaurant. Charlie was very excited. He announced that he had gotten an entry-level position at one of the big tech companies in San Francisco. He planned to get his master's and this would be a great opportunity. His moving to California was exciting too. Laura went through the motions to support her brother, but her heart was broken. I meant nothing to him, she thought. Just an opportunity. I have given away my virginity, sinned, and shamed myself for nothing. How could I be so stupid to think he cared anything about me? I have let everyone down, especially myself. "Are you OK, honey?" her mom asked. "You seem off today. It's a happy day for the family, but you are sad". "I'm fine, Mom. I think I'm sad because Charlie will be moving away". Laura put on a smile and tried to be interested in the conversation, but all she thought about was going to confession.

The next month was very busy. Charlie and his dad went to California. Dad stayed a week. Charlie went to job orientation and got settled in a tiny apartment near work. Dad raved about how the tech company would be a great place for Charlie to start his career. Laura waited until dad got home to tell her parents that she wanted to hold off a year on going back to school. Mom was very upset. "Why?" she demanded. "You are talented and you need to be in school. There is no reason for you to be home. You have not been yourself for a while now. What is going on?" She assured her mom that she was fine, but her mother persisted. "Sometimes we need a little help navigating life, Laura. I know a very caring therapist that you could see. Why not talk to her before you make any decision not to go back to school?" Laura could not imagine telling anyone about her indiscretion. "Not now, Mom. Really, I'm OK. Maybe later this summer." Her real worry now was that her period was late. She went to the library and searched for info on pregnancy symptoms. She thought you could not get pregnant on your first sexual encounter but found out that she was wrong. She had no morning sickness and hadn't gained any weight. She was hoping stress was the cause of her lateness. She had gone to confession and thought she would feel relieved, but she didn't. Dad cheerfully asked if he could take his 2 girls to dinner, but she just couldn't. She said she had a headache and went to her room to lie down. Her thoughts raced. She thought about talking to Randy, but why bother? He didn't even remember. He might even accuse her of lying. She just couldn't tell her parents and see the disappointment on their faces. They would forgive her and support her, but their relationship would never be the same. What about bringing a baby into the home? Her mom was so fragile it would be too much. Dad would demand to know who was the father and then would confront Randy. It would turn ugly quickly because he didn't remember. Then the demand for DNA and then a paternity suit. She cried until she was numb. She felt a new resolve. I'm going to stop this until I find out. Maybe I'm not pregnant. She would go tomorrow and get a test and know for sure what she was facing. She applied some makeup and went downstairs and told her parents she felt better and wanted to go to dinner with them. She knew they were pleased.

The next day was a crushing blow. She was definitely pregnant. She had gone to the library and used the restroom to take the test. She used 2 of them by different manufacturers, but the result was the same. She wandered around aimlessly all day. Mom wasn't doing well today. She said she wanted to rest and Laura heard her on the phone moving up her doctor's appointment. How could she tell them? She sat on a bench near the park and thought about going away and giving up the baby for adoption, but she knew her parents wouldn't hear of it. She glanced at a nearby bench and saw an ad for a Planned Parenthood Clinic. I couldn't, she thought, I would burn in hell forever. Maybe I could just get some information. She jotted down the phone number. She walked back to the library. They had a phone that allowed local calls and she didn't want to use her cell phone. The first time they answered, she hung up. She called back and asked some basic questions. They told her about medication that could be used if she was in the proper time frame. She decided she needed more information and made an appointment for the next day. As she was walking home, she passed her church. How could she ever go to church again? Father Karl was pulling out of the driveway to the rectory. He saw Laura and waved. If she did this, she could never confess to him. She had known him since her First Communion. She would find a church where no one knew her. Maybe she could seek forgiveness, but doubted that she could ever be forgiven for such a grievous sin.

When she got home Mom said that she had just returned from the doctor and he wanted her to come to the hospital for some tests. "Are you OK, Mom? What's wrong?" Her mom smiled. "It's ok, honey. Don't worry. The doctor didn't like a couple of test results and he wants to look into it. I go in tomorrow and I may not have to stay. I'm going to rest right now". That made the decision for her. She could not tell mom and dad. She went to her room and prayed for forgiveness. I am such a hypocrite, she thought. I'm only thinking of myself. What about this innocent baby? The tears flowed again, but she knew what she had to do.

Mom went to the hospital the next day and had to be admitted for more tests and a trial of some new medication. Laura kept her appointment at the Clinic and found out she was eligible for the medication. She went through a counseling session, an ultrasound and an examination, but was told she would have to come back another day to get the medication. They gave you time to be sure this was what you wanted to do. She stopped by the church on the way home and went in to pray. I wonder if I will ever be able to come in here again, she thought. When she got home Dad was getting ready to go see Mom. "Laura, I think I'm going to take mom to a nice resort to rest for a couple of days next week. A change of scenery and a little pampering might be good for her. Are you OK here"? She assured him she was fine and thought it was a good idea for mom. It also solved her other worry. She wondered what excuse she could use for lying around with stomach pains for a day. One less lie. What kind of person had she become? A liar, a betrayer of her faith, and soon a murderer.

The plan worked well. Laura went back and picked up the medication with full instructions. Mom was feeling better and stronger on the new meds. She and dad left for a few days stay at a lovely restful resort nearby. Laura went to the store and picked up all the supplies she would need and took her first pill. She had read everything thoroughly and knew what to expect. The pain was pretty intense after the second pill. She felt she deserved even more pain for what she was doing. After it was over, she had expected intense relief, but that didn't happen. She felt even more guilt and regret. Maybe she should have waited. Maybe she should have confided in Charlie. She could have gone to California and stayed with him. Catholic Charities could have found adoptive parents. One thing she would do for sure was go to confession. Surely that would bring some peace.

Ron and Susan had a relaxing time at the resort. They had discussed the change in Laura and were worried about it. She had not been seeing her friends and she still talked about not returning to school in the fall. Susan said she thought they should press her to get counseling. Ron didn't like the idea. He thought this was a phase and maybe related to Charlie moving away. They decided to call Charlie and ask him to spend some time talking to her. Laura had gone to confession at a church on the other side of town. The priest had been very stern and lectured her. He did give her absolution, but she felt she disgusted him. Mom and dad were really pushing her about school, but she just wasn't interested now. It would have to wait. She went online and found websites describing methods to deal with accepting guilt and moving on. One day when she was feeling especially low, she wrote a letter in her diary to her unborn baby. She explained why she did it and pleaded for forgiveness. It didn't help. In fact, she felt worse. Then Charlie called her and asked her to come for a visit. That sounded really good. Maybe she needed a change of pace. Mom and dad were very encouraging and Dad got her a room at a hotel near Charlie's apartment. She went for a week. She had really missed her brother and she had fun. She thought several times about telling Charlie, but she couldn't do it. He would be loving and supportive, but he would never look at her the same. He pushed for her to move there. She could go to school, get a part-time job and be near him. He would help her. He told her they were all worried because she had become sad and unhappy. She knew she couldn't leave Mom and she doubted that she would feel any different once the newness wore off. She knew her family loved her, but they couldn't cure the ache deep in her heart. She went home promising to visit again.

She did not return to school and Mom was insisting that she see a counselor. She was thin as a rail and practically lived in her room. It was turning into an ongoing argument. She insisted that she was fine and just needed time on her own. One day Laura told her mother that she was going to do a major cleaning of Susan's bedroom and bath. Drawers, closets, everything. Mom thought that might be a good sign. She helped by sorting through clothes and drawers. It was a good day. They chatted the whole time and the room really needed it. There were boxes of medications old and new that Susan had used through the years. Laura told her to go through all of them and get rid of the expired ones. She had bought her mother a handy med caddy and arranged her cabinet. When Ron came home, he was pleasantly surprised. Mostly because Laura was actually smiling and spending time with her mother. Plus, the room looked great. It was very organized and everything was cleaned. He went out and picked up dinner. Two days later Laura didn't come down for breakfast, which wasn't unusual. When she didn't come down for lunch, Susan was concerned. She called to her, but there was no answer. She went to her room and knocked. Nothing. She went in and Laura was lying on her bed. She was very pale with blue-tinged lips. Susan ran to her and shook her, but she was unresponsive. Laura's phone was next to the bed. She grabbed it and dialed 911, but in her heart, she knew it was too late. That was when she noticed the pill bottles on the nightstand. There were several of them that contained a variety of heart medications and sedatives that she had taken through the years. She pulled Laura into her arms and cried "No" and "Why" over and over. The emergency crew came in and pulled Susan away, so they could tend to Laura. Neighbors came when they saw the rescue truck. Soon Ron was there and Susan had to be sedated. Everything was in turmoil, but there was one certainty. Their beautiful, kind, shining light was no more.

Charlie paced around the hotel room with the memories stoking his anger. It had been over 17 years that Laura had been gone and almost 3 years since he found out the truth. The last time he saw Randy was at Laura's funeral. It was a heartbreaking time that carried very painful memories. Charlie had rushed home from California. Dad was still in shock and mom barely made it through. She tried hard to thank all the friends and family who came to the service, but she was heavily sedated. Randy attended with his family and they were very supportive. He remembered Randy asking quietly if he had any idea what happened. He said he saw her at our graduation and she had seemed fine, but Charlie had no answers. Because she died at home, there had been an autopsy. All anyone could say was "Why?" She had left a note on her desk. It was very brief and answered no one's questions. "Dear Mom, Dad, and Charlie. Please forgive me. I cannot forgive myself. I have brought shame to all of you, myself, and my faith. I love all of you, but I cannot live with this pain and shame. All my love, Laura." That was it. What shame? What pain? We knew she had changed over the summer, but we did not know why. He stayed for 3 weeks but had to get back to California to his job and classes for his master's degree. Before he left, the report came back from her autopsy. Mom and dad wouldn't even look at it. He read it thoroughly and was shocked to see that she had a recent pregnancy. How could that be? She didn't have a boyfriend. Could she have been raped? He discussed it with dad and he said not to tell mom. She could barely function. "Just leave it alone," he said. It doesn't matter anyway. Nothing does. It's my fault." Dad kept blaming himself for failing to recognize how depressed Laura had been. "Dad, it's no one's fault. Mom begged her to get counseling. Lots of young girls go through emotional times, but don't do anything like this. It is not your fault." He ended all conversation with the same thing. "I should have done more and been there for her."

Charlie went back to California and finished his master's in internet technology. He did very well and a number of firms were interested in him. He had been home a few times and could see his mother failing more each time. He decided to accept a position with a Cyber Security company outside of Hartford. It would be almost an hour's commute, but he could move home. His parents needed him. Susan lived almost a year after Laura passed away. She died with a broken heart and he stayed on living with dad. After a few months, Charlie approached his dad about dealing with both Laura's and Mom's things. Ron did not want to touch anything, but Charlie knew that was not a good environment. Dad finally agreed to clean Laura's room and convert it to a guest room, but he wouldn't touch any of mom's things. There were 2 cousins that lived fairly close and Charlie enlisted their help in dealing with Laura's room and they were great. They donated as much as they could to different organizations. When they finished, there were 2 large boxes of what they said were personal or special items that they thought should be looked through. They took those down to the basement with Laura's name on them. Since they were there, he really tried to convince Ron to let them deal with at least some of mom's things. He let them remove her things from the bathroom, but that was it. He just wasn't ready.

Chapter 17

Charlie had a few relationships, but it always came down to him putting his dad first, and the romance would be over. Fortunately, he loved his job. The internet was now becoming mainstream for home use and was a wide-open highway of opportunity. Along with the good came the bad. Hackers and ID theft had become a growing problem. His company was on the cutting edge of cyber security. Government entities and businesses were already seeing that new and stronger methods were needed to protect their data. It was exciting and challenging and he was glad it kept him so busy. Ron lived almost 4 years and died suddenly from a major stroke. Charlie was home and dad was in the kitchen. He heard a thump and a cry and ran to him. Ron struggled to say something as Charlie tried to lift him from the floor. "My fault, Charlie. It was my fault." And he passed away. In his dying breath, he blamed himself. Another funeral. He knew he had to get away. One of the neighbors had a brother who wanted to move to the area. They had approached him about renting the house. His cousins came back and this time cleaned out the whole house.

They did a great job and he was very grateful. There were a few boxes with personal effects from mom and dad, along with the original boxes from Laura that they put in the basement. The tenant said to leave them as it was not a problem. Charlie bought a townhouse much closer to Hartford and settled into a different lifestyle. Over the years he had a few relationships including a 3-year marriage that didn't work out. And then almost 3 years ago something changed. The man who was still renting the family home had passed away and his wife was moving. Real estate was selling pretty well, so he decided it was time to sell the house. He went there to evaluate how much work it would take to get it market-ready. He walked through the house with a notepad and thought about how well the tenants had cared for it. Paint, some fresh landscaping, and a bit of update to the kitchen and baths. When he went to the basement, the boxes from mom, dad, and Laura caught his eye. They were the boxes of personal items that his cousins had packed. He didn't want to dredge up old feelings and thought he would just toss them, but he couldn't do it. There might be something he should keep. He went through mom and dad's boxes and did find a few things that brought back happy memories. He dreaded looking at Laura's things. He found a couple of items he knew she treasured and put them aside. On the bottom of the box were several small books. They were dated diaries written over a number of years. He didn't know she had kept a diary and he put them with the other things. As he unpacked these he was drawn to the last diary. It was dated the year that she died. It seemed so invasive to read it, but maybe the book would shed some light on her tragic end. It was a typical young girl's writing over the year. She didn't write much each day unless there was something going on that was important to her. Her love of family and church was very strong and so was her total infatuation with Randy. He remembered her having a crush on him, but he hadn't realized how strongly she felt about him. She knew she was going to see him at the party and thought maybe it would be a turning point. She believed they were meant for each other and sooner or later they would be together. And then he read about the party. It was Randy who had gotten her pregnant and then brushed her aside at graduation. She had written "He told me to 'never settle for mediocrity'. It made me feel like he was leading a pep rally. I was never anything more than one of his fans". It broke his heart to read how she felt that she had no one to turn to. What kind of brother was he that she couldn't come to him? He had failed her. It sickened him to read about the abortion and the pain she was suffering inside. The priest admonishing her when she went to confession angered him. But the worst was her last post. She wrote a letter to her unborn baby. "My darling child. I have failed you. I have no right to even call myself your mother. A mother protects her young and I have destroyed you. All I can do is ask your forgiveness. I am a weak selfish person that could not stand up for you. I know God loves you. Forgive me." Anger and frustration overcame him. First, it was directed at himself, then the church, and then Randy. He could not get it out of his mind. After days of reflecting and rehashing, he came to an acceptance. His first thought had been to confront Randy and let him know what he had done, but he decided against it. Randy didn't know. He treated her as a kid with a crush. He did take advantage of her, but it was consensual. He was drunk and high, but that was no excuse. He had not seen or talked to Randy since her funeral. He wasn't even sure where Randy was living or what good would it do to make any accusations? He was torn. He had lost his whole family because of Randy. However, she had not told him and maybe he would have done something if she had. In his heart he knew Randy pretty well. He would not have done anything that hindered his career. DNA would have made him pay support, but he would not have been there with emotional support. He decided to let it rest because Randy didn't know. It was a bitter pill, but he swallowed it. He got very drunk that night and, in the morning, he felt he had made the right decision. Who knows? Maybe Randy didn't end up with the successful life he had always planned for himself. He kissed the diary and put it in the stack he was keeping.

That was over 2 years ago. He had done an internet search and found that Randy was a plastic surgeon living in Orlando. He had done a plastic surgery residency in Miami, married a Florida woman and had 2 children. He kept telling himself that he did the right thing by not confronting him, but there was a little place inside of him that ached. It ached for the pain and heartache of his whole family. Each of them destroyed by one careless act of an irresponsible egotist.

He had been with his company a long time and was on their long-range planning committee. A seminar was being held in Orlando and the company wanted him to attend. He came for 4 days and it was the second day that he saw the billboard. Now here he was, pacing in his hotel room. He pulled out his laptop and found the website listed on the billboard. A beautiful facility came up showing the professional interior. There was a surgical suite and a full spa. He clicked the tab About Us. There was Randy looking a bit older, but very much the same. He had an attractive-looking staff. Of course, everything would be perfect. He looked at the entire website. Someone had done a very good job. He closed his laptop and decided he would drive by the facility tomorrow.

After the seminar, Charlie found the surgical center. He parked across the street just to observe. It was a nice building on a tree-lined street and there was a lot of activity. There were several cars in the parking lot and people entering and leaving the building. There was a sign over one door that said Spa Entrance and another larger door with Randy's name. He had obviously spent a lot of money on getting the best. He toyed with the idea of a surprise visit, but dismissed it. He was never one to act hastily and he needed to sort out his feelings when he got home. He saw a medical supply truck delivering boxes and several women coming out of the spa laughing and talking. Somehow it all angered him. Then 2 women came out of the clinic door. The younger one was holding the arm of the older one. They were laughing and chatting. He had to leave. That could have been his mom and Laura spending time together. It was too much. He called and moved up his flight to tomorrow right after the last lecture. He couldn't stand being here another minute. He had seen enough.

Chapter 18

Charity Leveled and the team came back to meet with the office group. It was time for another update and make changes to the marketing plan. Randy was very pleased with the results so far. There were multiple cases every surgical day and patients were scheduling a month or more in advance. Charity had a couple more speaking engagements for him and suggested that he could start backing off some marketing as he was getting great word of mouth. She suggested keeping social media, and local magazine ads and not renew the billboard when the lease ran out. We were booked solid for the holiday season, but Randy did agree to take a long weekend over Thanksgiving. Hospital call had become too much and Mitch was happy to take all the days. Randy had never been one to talk much about his family life. He and his wife were still separated, but he saw his children regularly. He had rented a very nice townhouse with plenty of room for them to stay with him. Many people rant and rave about their ex, but he rarely talked about her. As close as Pam was to him, she knew little about his home life. My family was coming to visit me over Thanksgiving. Holidays are so hard when you have lost someone. It would be very difficult without David and I knew it would help having them here.

One afternoon after surgery Randy called me into his office. "Read this letter and tell me what you think," he said. It was from a young man in Wisconsin. He had sent photos of himself and photos of Lisa Marie Presley when she was a young woman. It was handwritten and had poor grammar. He was asking if Randy could do surgery on him to resemble her. He seemed sincere, but it was pretty bizarre. There were a lot of Elvis impersonators, but why Lisa Marie? "What do you think? Could it be some kind of scam? How does he even know you?" I asked. "I have no idea. For the sake of professionalism, I'm going to have Pam call him. At least we followed through." A few days later I asked Pam if she had called the guy. "You mean Franklin" she said. "I know it sounds crazy, but the guy seems very sincere. He said he had always loved the way Elvis looked and Lisa Marie looked like him, but with softer features. He was polite and asked for all the information regarding the surgery. He said he wants to schedule for the first of the year." I had learned by this time not to try to figure out anyone's motivation. I judged no one. My job was to keep them safe and comfortable. I had to admit that I was curious about Franklin.

We were very busy right up to December 23. Pam was getting calls about the Brazilian butt lift. Randy had done some research and told Pam he had decided not to offer them. "They are too risky, even at the hospital," he said. "I'm not comfortable doing them and the complication rate is too high". We were glad. They were a complex procedure. We were finishing early and Pam came back looking upset. "Will everyone please stay after the case? I need to talk to everyone." We gathered in Randy's office later and Pam told us that she had received a call that morning. "Remember Millie Robbins?" she asked. Randy immediately piped up "Sure. That is the 80-year-old lady we did the bleph (eye lid surgery) on. Is she alright?" "Oh, she's fine and happy," Pam said." She called to thank us for the lovely letter we sent telling her how proud you are to have her for a patient". Randy looked puzzled. "That sounds like a good thing. What's wrong with that?" "We didn't send a letter" Pam replied. "I remember you sending a letter" Teri suggested.

"That was a general happy holiday greeting we sent early in December. Charity had mentioned keeping it generic since we have patients of all faiths, but it can be a reminder for anyone wanting to get something done using their prepaid medical accounts or for the holidays. This was not our letter" Pam insisted. "Do you think she called the wrong office?" I wondered. We agreed that none of us had anything to do with a letter and that she had probably been mistaken. We were all glad that he had decided to close the week between Christmas and New Year's. Everyone had been working long days and we needed a break. The spa stayed open and was booked solid. Many gift certificates were sold and people were using them.

Everyone came back rested and looking forward to a busy year. A couple of days later Pam told me that Franklin was scheduled. I wanted to go over his health history and especially his meds, if any. When I finished the schedule, I called him. I don't know what I expected, but he sounded like a very pleasant young man who knew exactly what he wanted. "I'm concerned about your post-op care," I told him." "This is a big surgery and you will need help after. You will spend the first night here with our recovery nurse, but then you will be in a hotel. That's what I'm concerned about". "Don't worry" he said. "My brother will be with me. I don't know about staying overnight at your place though. My brother told my mom that he would be with me all the time. Can he stay with me there?" It was an unusual request, but I told him I would check and Pam would let him know. How weird, I thought. I hope his brother is a responsible person. I ran it by Randy and he said it was OK. We have had a few patients who did not speak English and someone else stayed overnight to act as a translator. Randy told Pam to expect a call from Tom's friend, Buddy Baker, the outrageous local radio morning host. Randy had seen him over the holidays and Buddy said he wanted to broadcast from Randy's office as he went in to have a liposuction. Randy told him he would only be able to be on air until he was medicated. Buddy said great. He thought it would be good publicity for him. Pam rolled her eyes and said she would work out the details. I thought this was going to be an interesting year. It had just begun and we had Franklin and Buddy in the wings. Little did I know just how interesting.

I arrived early on the day of Franklin's surgery. I wanted to allow plenty of time to speak to his brother. When I pulled in, I saw a totally beat car with Wisconsin plates in the parking lot. That was another question. Why would a person be getting this expensive surgery when his car was falling apart? I immediately checked his recent blood work and clearances and set up my anesthesia tray. He is a young strong guy and I was thinking that I should talk to Randy about adding another drug to our supply list. Fentanyl is a good anesthesia drug, but there was another one I liked better for certain cases. After set up I went in and met Franklin. I was surprised, but shouldn't have been. Here was a very clean-cut young man, who immediately stood up and came over and shook my hand. He was very pleasant and sincere. After we went over his history and talked about recovery, I had to ask him. "Franklin, you are spending a lot of money for this surgery. Do you hope to be a performer"? "Oh no, mam," he said. I only sing in the choir at my church." I felt compelled to ask him "Are you sure this is something you really want"? "Yes, mam. I have prayed about this a lot and I know this is what I want to do." I didn't understand, but it was his choice. His brother was the surprise. He was a tall, dark unsmiling middle aged man who seemed disinterested. He listened as I went over post-anesthesia instructions, nodding now and then. He said very little but was very specific that he would be staying overnight with his brother. I told him the surgery would be several hours and that he was free to get something to eat and come back later. He said he was fine and would not leave his brother. It just seemed strange to me. I mentioned it to Randy and asked if he thought it was strange. He shrugged and said if he stopped operating on strange people, he wouldn't have much work. The case was long but went well. I checked Franklin before I left for the day. His face had a full dressing, but he was awake and reasonably comfortable. His brother was sitting in the waiting room reading. I heard later that he had spent the week in Orlando and looked really good when the dressings were removed. He spent the night in the recovery room and his brother would not leave. Pam called him a few days after he was home and he said he was very pleased. She called a few days after that to ask him to send photos as he healed. His phone was no longer in service. She called emergency numbers he had filled out on his paperwork and the number for his brother. None of them were working. Randy said to send a certified letter asking how he was doing. It was returned as not deliverable. We all talked about it off and on for a few months and we had no answers. What happened to Franklin? One day as I watched a rerun of Goodfellows, it hit me. Could it be witness protection? I heard they would do surgical procedures to change someone's looks, but did they come up with such crazy background stories? We had a few flamboyant off the wall patients, but that was not Franklin. Nothing else made sense. The other thing that bothered me was his brother. He was anything but brotherly. I think that was an agent or marshal assigned to be with him at all times. We never knew for sure, but we hoped all was well.

Chapter 19

As our caseload increased, I felt that some of our patients would do better if we used a different anesthesia drug. I suggested to Randy that we get Sufentanil. I used it at the hospital a lot and thought it much better for the bigger and longer cases. It is 7-10 times more potent than Fentanyl, so it has to be administered differently. Patients wake up with less pain, are able to move better and it also has less nausea. Randy agreed that he liked the way patients woke up when it was used at the hospital and told me to order whatever I needed. I especially liked it for men, tummy tucks, and big liposuctions. Teri ordered it and the labels for the syringes.

The following Tuesday was a full day. Around noon Pam came back to the OR very concerned. She said that Nancy, from the spa, had gotten a couple of calls from previous patients who wanted to schedule their free facials. No one knew anything about free facials. She asked if any of us knew what was going on. Randy told Pam to find out who the patients were and get to the bottom of it. "What the hell is going on," he said. One of the patients who had called lived nearby and told Pam that she would bring in the letter that she received. Pam used some excuse to see it because she didn't want the patient to think we didn't know what was happening in our office. By the time we finished cases, Pam had a copy of the letter. It was on our letterhead thanking the patient for having surgery with us and offering her a free facial in our spa. Randy was very upset and said that someone must have hacked our internet. He called Charity and asked if someone could have done this through the marketing company. She said no, but thought we should immediately get a new internet service. She said she had clients that required very high security and she would find out the name of a strong local cyber security firm. Randy paced around the office wondering what else was out there. How many people were going to come in for freebies? What else had been compromised? Within the hour Charity called back. She had pulled some strings and we were getting an emergency visit from a top-notch security firm. They had contracts with financial institutions and government agencies, so she was confident they could help us. Randy and Pam stayed to meet them and the rest of us left for the day. We were all very concerned.

The next day was a bad one for the patient consults. The internet was completely shut down as the company was working on our system. Patients wanted to schedule surgery, but Pam could not pull up any dates without the computer. She had printed out a calendar last week, so she tried giving patients tentative dates. People seemed to understand that we had internet problems, but it made us look disorganized. So far 5 women have scheduled free facials. Randy was the most upset because there was not a clear answer as to who did this. Dalton Davis, who was our contact from the security firm, said that most of the time it is very difficult to find out who hacked into your computer. He said they were checking all of our contacts and they were installing new firewalls. He felt the new system would protect us. By the end of the day, we were up and running. We all got new passwords and new login info. Randy asked Dalton if he thought this was a personal attack. "It's hard to say," Dalton said. "Has someone threatened you"? Randy said no, but there was a lot of professional jealousy. He had become one of the busiest plastic surgeons in town in a short time, but he couldn't think of anyone who would do this. Dalton added "This could be someone sitting around stirring up trouble for you for no reason. They may not even know you. People do this for entertainment. Although I have to admit that this free facial thing is a new one on me". He suggested that all of us in the office change our passwords at home and let him know if we noticed anything unusual on our home computers. Pam got a couple of calls from vendors that couldn't reach us and called Charity because social media had the wrong website listed. They were already working on it. By the end of the week, things had settled down and Randy was less anxious. There had been no more calls for the free facials so we hoped this was over.

A couple of weeks went by and Buddy Baker was scheduled for his liposuction. It was on a Friday, so no one else was there. He brought in his crew and broadcast from the office. He made jokes about how he was leaving his fat ass here and he shared everything being done on air. He got lots of calls asking questions. When it came time for sedation, I had already warned everyone that was the end for him being on air. As my pre-op cocktail kicked in, he said his goodbyes, and his sidekick took over the show. He had a successful liposuction and looked really good. Randy got several patients from the broadcast.

January was busy, but not crushing busy. We finished early one afternoon and Pam had ordered lunch for us. While we were eating, she said she had a surprise. "We will be seeing one of our favorite patient supporters. Lonnie Gretsky is coming back." I piped up with "Is one of them having a redo?" "Nope." She said. "It's a new one. And I asked about his wife and girlfriend and he said they were all fine." Randy said, "Remember the rules of confidentiality." "Are you sure he isn't joking?" Teri asked. "I think his payment in full answers that question," Pam replied. Someone asked, "How many do you think he has?" As Randy was leaving, he said "His personal life is none of our business. We treat everyone the same. Hopefully, he will return to us for any of his cosmetic needs. He is already talking to me about having a bleph." Someone else said, "Do you think he will bring donuts?" That got a laugh from all of us.

Toward the end of January trouble started. Nancy came over from the spa and said that she was getting multiple calls about scheduling a free facial for the Valentine's Day Patient Appreciation Gift. Pam was upset. "How many?" she asked. Nancy said she had stalled everyone by saying that a special schedule had to be completed and she would get back to them. There had been 7 calls that day and it was only 1:00. They dreaded telling Randy. He was livid. "Get me a copy of the letter from someone and get me Dalton Davis on the phone now. I paid a ton to that cyber security firm and I get this bullshit. Also, get Charity on the phone and cancel that billboard now. It might be aggravating someone." He slammed the door as he went into his office. Dalton was able to go into our internet remotely and called to say that he saw emails sent through an entity on our admin list, not our regular patient mailing. Tracking it was a dead end. It had sent the letters and then deleted itself. He said he would come over and look at some things on our computers. The really bad news was that it looked like 20 letters had been sent. Randy had a few consults to see and he tried hard to be pleasant. Dalton arrived and spent time with Pam going over computer files and looking for names she didn't recognize. It was difficult. They dealt with many entities and the online names were not always familiar. He said he thought someone had hacked into the system and was hiding behind a familiar account name. They removed a lot of names and he said he was going to verify every one of the names left. After the last patient, he went in to talk to Randy. There was a lot of shouting and Randy left the office in a huff. Dalton said he would be in touch after they had done more work. "Can you tell these ladies that it was a computer error?" he asked. Pam shook her head. "No. We would look really bad and disorganized. Who wants to go to a surgeon who can't keep his office organized? Someone would have that on social media in 10 minutes. This will cost around $2000." Dalton shook his head. "I'll do my best to get to the bottom of it".

Chapter 20

Charlie Devon walked down to his basement eating a sandwich. He had a great setup. There were 4 computers all used for different reasons. It was very expensive, but his main interest. One had special security that he used for work projects. One was a very high-tech gaming machine that he used to play with gamers around the world. One was his home base that he used to pay bills, keep in touch with friends and all normal computer uses. The last one was for "special projects". He had set it up with emails of various bogus company names for medical supply places and with various combinations of Randy's name. They were all set up to be used once and then self-delete. The web address names would not draw general scrutiny. He wanted nothing from Randy. He wanted him to be anxious, worried, unhappy and afraid of the future, just as his parents and Laura had felt. From the time Randy was a kid, he always had to be in control. He had to be the leader, the president, the front man. If he wasn't in control, he would find a way to manipulate the situation, so he would get his way. He always had to be right and that was his Achilles heel. When he was not in control, he made bad decisions. Charlie had seen this all through Randy's young life and he was sure that he had not changed. As he scrolled through the computer files, he could see that some had been removed and the one sending the Valentine's gift had deleted itself. 20 ladies would get a nice facial. Randy can afford it. He had access to his financial records too and he was making a lot of money. He hoped to see that income down by the time he was finished with him.

Mitch called me over the weekend and invited me to dinner. As soon as he picked me up, I knew something was bothering him. When we were seated and had ordered a drink, I asked what was going on. "I went to dinner Friday night with Randy," he said. "He had 2 drinks. I haven't seen him drink since he came back from rehab. He got defensive about it and said that strong people can have a drink now and then. He complained the whole meal that someone was out to get him and he was afraid this was just the beginning." "Oh no. I didn't know he was drinking" I said. "Do you think this internet thing could just be a one-off?" Mitch shrugged. "I can't think of anyone that would want to or even be capable of doing this. Randy has his share of professional jealousy and people that just don't like him, but this even has the security company stumped." "How do you think he would take the suggestion of going back to rehab, even for just a couple of weeks? I know other people that slipped back and were able to get back on track with a little help" I asked. Mitch pondered that. "He sounded really touchy when I just looked at his drinks, so I didn't say anything". On the way home I told Mitch that I was going to try to start a conversation and see where it went.

I didn't get the chance because Randy came in flying high. His aunt in New York City worked for a cable network that aired several women's interest channels and she got them interested in doing a show on cosmetic surgery. They were going to discuss types of cosmetic procedures with lots of photos and take call in questions. Randy would be the featured plastic surgeon. It got him off the subject of the internet situation for a while. He gave Pam a number to get him an appointment with a police detective. He had called a lawyer friend, who knew a lot of people in the police department and had lined up someone to talk to him. We tried to convince him to take the week off and stay up east and visit family when he finished the TV show. He said he would do a couple of days, but that is all. He said he needed to be working because the future was uncertain.

The next day as we were setting up surgery, we heard the booming voice of Lonnie Gretsky. Introductions all around, of course. He was holding 2 boxes of donuts. Stifling a smile, I peeked in the top box and there were 4 jelly-filled buns with icing. I winked at him and he winked back. The couple left happy with his privacy intact.

A few days later Randy came in gloomy and irritable. He had met with the detective and was told there wasn't much the police could do. There had been no physical harm to anyone. Randy said that it was a form of theft because he had to do the facials for free. The detective said no. Randy could have told the patients the truth and not done the procedures. It was Randy's choice to go ahead with them. It was fraud and illegal and he would refer everything to their cybercrime division, but he wasn't hopeful for any solution. Evidence was thin. The letters had been on Randy's letterhead and there had been no threats. In other words, they could not help. To make the day even worse, he had accidentally contaminated one side of the OR table and we had to do a completely new setup. He was yelling at Becky, but we all knew he had been at fault. As I was cleaning up, I saw Pam go into his office and come out looking upset. "Are you ok?" I asked. She pulled me aside. "When I went in, I knocked and just walked in like I normally do. I saw him quickly put something in his desk drawer. I think he is drinking." That was not good news. We looked at each other helplessly and wondered what we could do. Wes Ford came in then and told us that he was going to be gone for a few days and Zach would be doing our terminal cleaning. Pam made a face. Wes said, "I know you aren't crazy about him, but he will do a good job." He smiled "It's nice to know that I will be missed." Wes had been great. Even if we had long days and didn't finish until 7 or 8, Wes was there at the end of the day. Pam said, "I'm not going to put up with any crap from Zach. He's sneaky and I'm not going to leave until he's done. Do not give him your key. I don't trust him". Wes assured us that he would not give Zach a key and he would have a strong talk with him before he left. It worked out that the first week would only be one surgery day because

Randy would be in New York for the show, so Pam was glad for that.

The show was done live with an audience. We all met at the office and watched together. Randy was in his element. He was handsome, charming and brilliant. He handled all the questions and his explanations were very clear. The women on the show were all fawning over him. We didn't see it on the show, but he told us that afterward there were reporters from several magazines wanting interviews. Of course, he was very accommodating. It gave him a break from the office worries.

Dalton Davis had been back to see Pam. He said he was checking our system regularly and he thought this might be coming from outside the U.S. It was very difficult to nail anything down. Even the FBI and the Pentagon had issues with hackers. Some were caught, but many were not. He told us to change our office and personal passwords regularly and he asked how many ladies took advantage of the Valentine facials. "All of them," Pam said. "You can't blame them," he said. We agreed.

Randy came back to work still in a great mood from the show. He slowly started drifting into an agitated state. He didn't appear to be drinking. One day as I was leaving work, I noticed Randy outside his side door talking to Zach. I thought it was odd because Randy never used that door and he had spoken to Zach in his office earlier. Maybe I'm just paranoid because I don't like Zach. Wes was back next week, so this was the only day with Zach. It bothered me that Randy was talking to him secretly.

When I got home Mitch called me. "Can I stop by?" he asked. "Sure. Come on over" I said. He looked down and upset. "Randy blew up at me last night. We went to dinner, so he could give me the lowdown on the TV show. He had 2 double scotches and I had to say something. I was not accusatory or negative, just concerned. He really overreacted. Told me to fuck off and mind my own business. He was fine and didn't need advice from anybody. He threw some money on the table and stormed out." I hated hearing that and told him about the meeting I saw with Zach. "Who is Zach?" he asked. "He's a terminal cleaner who works with Wes and he's a shady guy," I said. "He goes way back with Wes and he does a decent job, but we just don't trust him. He would be someone you could approach if you wanted to score something. Do you think it would do any good for me to try to talk to him?" Mitch was thoughtful. "Bide your time and try to gauge his mood. I wouldn't right now because he's really defensive. Maybe if this internet situation is resolved he will calm down". I was glad Mitch had told me, but what if it got worse? Pam knew him best. I would talk to her tomorrow and see what she thought.

Pam was concerned too. I shared what Mitch had told me about Randy's blowup. She said she had been worried because she called him on 2 separate occasions recently and he didn't return her call. He had never done that before. He had called her early the next morning and apologized. He said he fell asleep and didn't hear his phone.

The next surgery day we were really busy. Randy came in very upbeat. He was joking with everyone and bought lunch for the surgery and spa staff. He said he was confident Dalton Davis would get to the bottom of the internet hack. We were getting a lot of publicity from the TV show. I didn't realize how many people watched these special interest afternoon cable shows. Pam came back to the OR and told us that she was booking consults 6 weeks out and surgery days were filling up fast. Randy loved it. He said he knew plastic surgeons in Manhattan who booked surgery 6-9 months in advance. "That's my goal" he laughed. We were all glad to see him happy and energetic.

Chapter 21

It was by chance that Charlie Devon read about Randy's TV appearance. There was a small local newspaper in his home town that he got once a week. It was local news only with obituaries, success stories, and local scandals. He had signed up for it years ago and had it on auto-pay. It kept coming and he still liked reading the local news now and then. There was a story about a local boy, who is now a successful Florida plastic surgeon, being featured on a TV network. Small towns love Local Boy Makes Good stories. They had a few pictures and lots of quotes from the show. Charlie was seething. His whole family was in the cemetery while Randy was hamming it up and probably generating lots of business. He was going to crank things up a bit. Randy needed to feel the insecurity and fear that Laura had felt.

Randy had been more like his old self for a couple of weeks. Mitch told me that Randy had invited him out to dinner and had apologized for his angry outburst. He did have one drink and claimed he was doing great, but Mitch was still concerned.

We were finishing surgery when Pam came back looking upset. "I need to see you as soon as you finish," she told Randy. As we were cleaning up and getting the patient to recovery, we heard yelling coming from Randy's office. Pam came out shaking her head and rolling her eyes. "This is bad," she said as she walked by. A patient who had been in for a consult for breast augmentation had just called. She was very excited that she had been "selected" to receive a free breast augmentation. She would have to pay for her medical clearance fees, but the surgery was free, including the price of the implants. Randy was livid and worried about how many others may have gotten such a letter. Pam said there had been no other calls, but she didn't know what to do. Randy called his lawyer and Dalton Davis. Dalton said he was escalating the problem to a higher security level in the company and would keep us posted. His lawyer told him that he could tell the patient that it was a scam by a hacker and he couldn't do free surgery. It was risky though. She might become angry and go to the press or social media. The fallout could be much more expensive than the free surgery. "But where does this end?" Randy asked. "I'm being held hostage". The lawyer agreed that he was. He said that there had to be someone with a grudge and he suggested a really strong private investigator to look over his background. Randy called his friend at the Orlando Police Department. "This is illegal," Randy told him. "It's theft. The normal fee is $5000. Can't I press charges?" The detective sympathized, but told him the truth. There was no one to charge. Of course, it is illegal, but no one knows who is doing it. You can stop it by shutting down your internet, but he had no other advice. Randy said he already had a cyber security firm monitoring his office, but had no luck finding the hacker. The internet is a whole new world of crime and the perpetrator is hidden. It can take months, even years, to catch someone hacking into highly secure networks. He suggested that Randy write a list of anyone who had any issues with him since moving to Orlando. A private detective could at least check them out. That would be a significant list, Randy thought. Success brings a lot of envy and professional jealousy. He made the list, even thinking of anyone he had met at rehab. He made an appointment with a private investigator recommended by his detective friend. By this time, he was very agitated and anxious. He wanted to get home and get one of the Xanax he had gotten from Zach. He had to calm down. His hands were shaking. Just a touch of his favorite scotch would help calm him until he could get home. He had a full day of surgery tomorrow and he had to get some rest.

Surgery the next day was stressful. Randy was crabby and on edge all day. Dalton came to the office and told Pam they were installing some new security in the system. He explained a 2-part security that would have to be done in order to send or receive any emails from the office. She said it sounded like a nightmare considering how many emails she sent. She had been telling Randy that she needed an assistant just to keep up with the scheduling and routine information requests. Dalton suggested she hold off a bit on bringing in anyone new until this problem was solved. "All problems eventually get solved," he said. Small comfort, thought Pam. When?

A few weeks later Randy did the free surgery and the patient was ecstatic. She left glowing reviews on multiple sites. Pam approached the implant company and was able to get a free pair of implants. Randy was pleased with that, but still irritable most days. Just when you think things can't get any worse, they often do. Randy was home after a long and tiring day. He had picked up dinner and sat down at his computer to check his emails. There were a couple of interesting seminars, a few jokes from friends and lots of spam. As he was deleting junk mail, one caught his eye. In the subject box, it said "Did you like free surgery"? What the hell is this, he thought as he opened the message. "It was so nice of you to give the free breast augmentation to that sweet girl. She is hardworking and deserved a break. Maybe I can find other deserving patients for free surgery. What a guy!" What the hell? He immediately hit Reply. "Who is this and what do you want? Why are you tormenting me?" He hit Send. An immediate reply came back. His message was undeliverable. He quickly tried to print out everything, but the message had disappeared. He called Dalton Davis. There was no answer, so he left an urgent message. He was shaking and angry. I'm not paranoid, he thought. There is someone who wants to destroy me. Why? He couldn't eat his dinner. The anxiety made him want to run out the door screaming, and he knew he had to calm down. He took a Xanax and poured some scotch. Thank God I don't have surgery tomorrow, he thought. I need to call Zach and get something stronger, just to get me through this. I need something to help me concentrate on my work. He thought about the Adderall he had taken during college. They had worked great. He would be careful and take just one when he did surgery. It really helped him focus before, but he did remember having trouble sleeping. He would take it early in the morning. He swore to himself that he would go back to rehab when this was over. Now that this bastard has made contact, they can catch him, he thought. He held his hands up to eye level and saw the nervous tremor. I'll be okay, he reassured himself as he gulped down the scotch and poured another.

On a non-surgery day, I was working around my house getting some cleaning done when Pam called me. She was upset and worried. Today was consult day and she said Randy was terrible. He came in 40 minutes late, which he never did, and he looked awful. He said he didn't sleep well, and he told her about the email. Dalton had called and said he got the message and was looking at Randy's home computer security. They had looked at all of the employee's home computers when they came in initially and he was able to check remotely. The email was gone and they were trying to trace the sender. Randy asked if he should cancel his home internet. Dalton said no because maybe the hacker would make a mistake and they would be able to trace him. He recommended removing all personal and financial information and storing it on an external hard drive. In today's world, security is much better. However, it can still be very difficult to trace a really knowledgeable hacker. Pam was also upset about how Randy looked. He would always dress well for consult day with a suit, tie and coordinated shirt. But today he looked thrown together. He also looked a little shaky, which was really upsetting. One patient commented that he wasn't very friendly and another said he hadn't explained the procedure well to her. "I tried to cover as best I could," Pam said. "This is new behavior and I really don't like it." The private investigator came near the end of the day. He was with Randy for over an hour. "When I left," Pam told me, "Randy was just sitting at his desk. He told me he didn't know what he was going to do. I have never seen him like this. I don't know what to do, Sunny. I have a really bad feeling about this."

I did too. I called Mitch to see if he could stop by for dinner. I wanted to brainstorm with him and didn't want to chance being overheard in a restaurant. Dinner was cooking and I handed him a drink when he came in. We sat in the lanai and I filled him in on the latest email. He said he knew a few people who hated Randy, but none had the technical ability to pull off this scheme. "Could someone hire a person to do this?" I asked. "I'm sure you can. If you have enough money, you can get just about anything done" he replied. "You know I have heard of the dark web and you can get any kind of services there. I'm going to mention it to Randy. Maybe his cyber team can look at it." We talked for an hour then had dinner. Mitch said he was going to put out feelers around the hospitals to see if anyone could remember someone cursing or threatening Randy. He didn't want to say too much because Randy wanted to keep this as quiet as possible. We both felt sad and helpless.

Chapter 22

The rest of the week was routine and the weekend was quiet. During Tuesday's consults, Randy told Pam he had run into a friend who was a banking executive, Bob Sorino. He wanted a facelift, but needed it to be done soon. "That might be hard," Pam said. "We are scheduled several weeks out". "I know you can figure out something, Pam. He's coming by this afternoon for a consult." Pam was surprised. "We are fully booked. I can't get him in today." Randy immediately became sulky and defensive. "Yes, you can. I don't want to lose a big case like this. Just do it." He started walking away. "What time is he coming?" Pam asked. "It's open" Randy replied, as he walked to his office. "Whenever he gets done at work". What the hell, Pam thought. Now he's screwing up the schedule. This would throw a monkey wrench in the whole afternoon. She mulled over the schedule and saw no opportunity for a face lift consult. That was a big surgery and both the consult and surgery took longer than most of the other procedures. The hell with it, she thought. I'll let his friend cool his heels in the waiting room until the end of the day. Of course, Bob arrived about 3:30 and expected to be shown right in. Pam had updated Teri about the unexpected patient and she kept the scheduled patients moving. Pam gave Bob the usual paperwork packet and brought him some water. After 10 minutes he came to Pam's desk and said "I don't need to fill out all this crap. Randy knows me. I'm sure he would say it's ok. How soon can I get in to see him?" Pam gritted her teeth, but smiled. "This paperwork is required by state regulations. Randy needs this to be sure you won't have any complications. He has approved all of this information, and he wants you to fill it out. It will just take a few minutes." Bob rolled his eyes and sat back down. A few minutes later he brought it back to Pam. "Here it is" he said. She glanced through it and saw the whole area about his general health had been skipped. "Mr. Sorino" she said. "You have missed a very important part of the questions. We need to know about your health and what medications you take." He was becoming impatient. "You can get all that stuff from my doctor. Just call them and tell them to send it over". "I can't do that, Mr. Sorino. You would have to sign a release with them. Also, we need to know your general health, so we can order the appropriate pre-op testing and clearances. Please just fill it out. Randy will need to see it". "Why are you making a big deal of this" he asked. "This is just cosmetic surgery". Pam was very aggravated, but she saw they were getting through the scheduled patients. "Mr. Sorino, this is major surgery with general anesthesia. It is just as serious as any other surgery you have. It will just take a few minutes. Please". With that he tossed the packet on Pam's desk and said "The hell with it" and walked out the door. The last patient waiting to go in looked at Pam and said "What's his problem? I know his type. He thinks he is more important than anyone else". Just then Randy opened the door and looked in the waiting room. He looked at Pam. "Did Bob come in?" he asked. Pam told him what happened. The patient waiting looked at Randy and said "That guy is trouble, Doc." Randy just smiled and said "He's very demanding, but he's a good guy. I'll call him and tell him to come back". "I'm next" the patient said. "You bet." Randy smiled and closed the door. Teri took her back to the consulting area and about 15 minutes later Bob was back. He immediately went to Pam's desk and said Randy had called him to come back and told him he didn't have to fill out any more paper crap. Soon Teri came to the door, looked at Pam, and rolled her eyes. "Come on back, Mr. Sorino". Pam was pissed. Breaking routine was always trouble. There are rules for a reason, and she intended to talk to Randy when good old Bob left. Randy walked to the front desk with Bob and called Teri and Pam over. "Bob wants to schedule a facelift," Randy said. "Send over a request from our office to his primary care for his medical records. We will get his history from there. Tell them we need medical clearance and give him orders for routine bloodwork". Pam was trying hard to be civil. "Does he have high blood pressure?" Teri asked. "If he does, Sunny will need electrolytes." "Well, Bob, do you?" Randy asked him. "Not much, Doc, but I do have some medication." Teri said "Your bloodwork must be within 3 days of your surgery. That is a rule." Randy patted him on the back and said we would get it all worked out. "Find him a day, Pam". She was already looking. She wanted to get him over with as soon as possible. There had been a cancellation 2 weeks ahead and she asked him if that would work. "You have to get your medical clearance though. Is that enough time for you?" "My primary care guy is a friend," he said.

"He will get me in". When he left, Pam tried to talk to Randy about Bob's attitude. "I wouldn't worry if he was a liposuction or a rhinoplasty, but this is a face lift. He is not going to be compliant". "Pam, my stress level is over the top right now. I'm just taking it day by day, waiting for the next bomb to drop. He's an influential guy. He's been bugging me for months to do this, and I just want to do it and get it over with. Please just go with the flow." "Randy, I'm worried about you. I've seen you under lots of stress and you always handle it. Maybe you should take time off. If we closed for a while, this ghost hacker might go away. Stress can cause poor decision-making. I am really worried". He looked dejected. "I'm worried about me too, Pam. Thanks for all you do".

The next couple of weeks went reasonably well. There had been nothing from the internet stalker. Dalton had been excited because they thought they had found something, but it went nowhere. Randy was in better form. He was more focused and energized and he seemed like his old self. He had met with Zach and decided to try Adderall. He had not used it a lot in med school, but when he did, it worked great. He decided to get it from Zach because he didn't want a record of him getting a prescription. With more energy and a clearer focus, he had cut back on alcohol. However, the Adderall sometimes kept him awake and he needed Xanax to sleep. The time he had taken Xanax with alcohol he had overslept and felt out of it all day. All of these drugs are only temporary, he told himself. Once I get rid of this stalker, I will take a rest, maybe go to rehab and get back on track. If I can find the right combo of meds, I can keep the stress in check. Just for now. This is everything I have dreamed about and worked for all these years, and I can't panic. Why is some asshole doing this to me? I'll kill the bastard if I find out who it is. He had taken one Adderall today. On big surgery days he would take a second one for the later afternoon cases. He felt focused and in control with surgery, but found he sometimes needed a second Xanax or he couldn't sleep. Since he only had one today, he was going to have just a touch of his favorite scotch. He knew he was getting it all under control.

The day came for Bob Sorino's face lift. It had been like pulling teeth to get all of the required pre-op work done. He had not shown up for his medical clearance appointment and it was done just 2 days before. We had not received the results of his bloodwork, but he assured Randy that it had been done. Pam wanted to take him off the schedule when he didn't show up for the clearance, but Randy wouldn't do it. I was hoping to find food crumbs or some evidence of his having eaten, so I could cancel him, but no luck. A lady friend came with him and said she was driving him home. Pam said "Are you staying with him afterward? He has to have a caregiver." She replied, "I offered to, but he said he would be fine and he didn't need me. I can stay, if you think it's necessary". This told us that he had not listened to one word of the instructions that Teri had given him. It was also in the written pre- and post-op instructions. You must have a care giver, rest with head elevated, cold packs, no chewing, no talking, quiet, regular examination of dressings for bleeding and swelling. He had not paid attention to anything. Pam said she would go over everything with her after they took him back to surgery. She did produce a copy of the bloodwork. I felt I needed to express my feelings to Randy. "This is a bad idea, Randy. He has been noncompliant from his first visit. He didn't even plan to have a caregiver. I think you should reconsider operating on him." "Do you have a solid reason for canceling him? Being unlikeable and a pain in the ass doesn't count," he said. "If I cancel him, he will come back until I do it. Ever since the TV show he has been hounding me. Let's just get him over with." We did the face lift. A face lift on a man is different than on a woman. A man has a strong blood supply to his beard. Think of just a tiny nick from shaving and how much it will bleed. It was a tedious case, but he did well. He had a small drain on each side behind the ear and a pressure dressing to help control swelling and bleeding. He woke up pretty mellow. I had used Sufentanil for anesthesia and he still had a numbing effect from the local, so he wasn't in pain. As he got more awake, his naturally demanding personality came roaring back. He wanted the pressure dressing off because it was too tight. He didn't like the drains and became agitated in general, so I gave him some sedation to calm him down. Randy came back to reassure him, but he kept pulling at the dressings and begging Randy to take it off. Randy finally gave in and told Teri to take it off and put on a simple dressing. He calmed down and dozed a bit. When his girlfriend came back to the recovery room she was in shock. "I had no idea he was going to look like this," she said. I went to Randy and suggested he put him in the hospital overnight. "This guy is a time bomb," I said. Randy replied "He won't want to pay for it. It's related to cosmetic surgery, so I don't know if his insurance will cover it. Also, I think he would refuse to go." "You pay for it, Randy. It would be worth the peace of mind. I bet this girlfriend is going to be on the phone with you all night. You will get no rest." "I'll see how it goes," he said. He gave the girlfriend a prescription for oral Valium to get filled now before she took him home. Teri gave him one from the office supply, and he was much calmer and behaving. He was tolerating the simple dressing and starting to make jokes. Randy came in and really stressed following all of the instructions to both of them. By the time they were leaving, he was steady on his feet and telling all of us how he was fine and this was no big deal. Teri and I just looked at each other. Pam knew this was going to be a hectic day, so she had kept it light. Randy only had to see some rechecks and do a couple of minor procedures. Mitch stopped by to book the room for a cosmetic case and asked Randy to dinner. As they were leaving Randy asked

Pam to call and check on Bob. Pam did and told Randy "He answered the phone". "What?" Randy was shocked. "Why is he talking? Where is the girlfriend?" Pam asked more questions. "She's there and she says he's been making calls". "Give me the phone". Randy gave Bob hell and told him he was going to ruin his surgery. Even worse, he could start bleeding, which is a hematoma. It is not only dangerous but can have lasting effects on the surgical result. Bob promised he would stop talking and relax. He said he was perfectly fine. Pam, Teri, and I gave Randy the old told-you-so look. Mitch looked bewildered. "What's going on," he asked. "You are seeing the results of not listening to your staff," Randy told him.

I was home enjoying a good book when my phone rang at about 8 p.m. Randy was very agitated. "Sunny, can you get to the office right away? I have to take Bob back to surgery". "What's going on?" I asked. "That damn fool went out to dinner. A steak dinner. He took his dressing off and put big band-aids over his drains. He was chewing steak and his face started to swell up on one side. His girlfriend told him he was swelling and he started having trouble swallowing. They called me and I told them to meet me at the office. Now it's the other side too. Bilateral hematomas. I'm going to have to find bleeders and redo the whole thing. Damn him. Can you get here right away? I thought about it for a minute. "Randy, I can't do it. He just ate. He has a full stomach and is high risk. He is not someone we can safely do in the office. Take him to the hospital." I thought he might be upset, but not at all. "You are right, Sunny. He can pay for the hospital and the hospital OR. He can find out what happens when you think you know everything." "Also," I said, "they can sedate him and keep his ass quiet for the next couple of days. What a damn fool. I hope he hasn't done any permanent damage." Randy sounded dejected. "I'm sorry I didn't listen to you, Teri or Pam. I was with Mitch when I got the call. He offered to scrub in and give me a hand. Check tomorrow and see how it went."

The next couple of weeks were tense. Bob was out of the hospital and doing well, but he was still bruised and his scars were not healing as well as we would have liked. We convinced Randy to take many photos and document everything he did and what Bob didn't do. Bob said he was pleased and didn't blame Randy for anything. Thankfully, he did not get any infection. Randy was irritable and grumpy most of the time, but kept busy.

Chapter 23

One morning a couple weeks later, he came in early for surgery and looked terrible. He called all of us into his office. He sat down and handed a sheet of paper to Pam. "Read this to everyone". Pam took the paper and said "It looks like a photo of an email." "It is" he replied. "I was able to snap a picture just before it disappeared from my screen". Pam read "It looks like you are keeping really busy, my friend. I'll bet the money is just pouring into your bank account. I wonder how your patients would feel if they read about their personal medical histories on the internet. I was thinking about the two women who work for the mayor. One takes an antipsychotic med and the other has herpes. What kind of support staff is that for a mayor? I haven't decided if I'm going to plant a few interesting facts on social media, but in the meantime, I think it would be nice for you to do a liposuction for a lucky person who listens to your friend, Buddy Baker. He was broadcasting live the day you did his liposuction, so he could choose a lucky recipient. I sent him an email, from you of course, telling him of your good idea for a promotion. He will love the publicity. Keep the money coming in. You're going to need it."

We looked at one another in shock. "My God," I said. "This is a real maniac, who needs to be in jail. What can you do?" "I didn't sleep a wink last night," he said. "But I really think there are some things we can do. Let's get through the surgeries today and afterward we can brainstorm some ideas." Randy perked up and we got through the cases. He had jotted down ideas all night long. He was not planning to tell the staff that his goal was to close this practice in a year. He knew he had the stamina to maximize his case load and get it to a peak. He could then sell it and the building. That would give him an opportunity to pursue a new way of life. There would be enough money to move, join a large practice or a university teaching program. He could walk away from all of the stress and threats. He didn't like the idea of not being his own boss, but he couldn't stand this much longer. A year is all he needed and he knew he could do it. In the meantime, he had come up with some ideas. "We can't control this person," he said. "We have to go another route. Pam, I want you to find a company that can store our patient information.

The patients would fill out their paperwork and we will find a way to forward it, but not on any of our internet servers. Get ahold of Dalton and ask him how we can do this. Pam, you and I are going to go to the bank and discuss a way that some patients can pay for their procedures directly to a bank account that does not go through our office. The spa is okay because they have limited patient information. We have to do something. Also, I want to ramp up business. We do surgery 3 days a week, but I know we could do 4. What do all of you think?" Pam spoke first. "I'm with you on anything to protect the privacy of our patients and limit the information this cyber thief can find. If you want to add another surgery day, we need more help. I will need someone to help me with whatever data system we come up with. It won't be as easy as it is now". Teri spoke next. "We will need a part-time nurse. Actually, we need one now. I need more time to do pre-op evaluations and make sure everyone is ready for surgery. That is along with the post-op checks and generally keeping everything running. I have been staying late just to keep up with 3 surgery days. I would like a nurse to come in at least 2 days a week." Claudia spoke next. "I can pick up the OR time and we can get a new recovery nurse. I know someone from the hospital. I can go between the OR and recovery to help wherever I'm needed." Becky said "I need the money, so I don't mind the extra day. I have been doing extra shifts at the hospital and I would rather do this". Randy agreed and was pleased with the response from his staff. "Now Sunny, what do you think? I really don't want anyone else to do my anesthesia, but I think I could get Bobby McFadden one day a week." I decided to be honest. "I am not crazy about Bobby and not because of his past. I know he is trying really hard since his drug problems, but this is not the environment he needs. In this setting there is nothing between the anesthesia provider and controlled drugs except your own integrity, and it would be a huge temptation. He is monitored in the hospital and knows he is accountable. I will do the extra day, but I do think that a salary adjustment may be in order for all of us. We have been here 2 years now, so I think it would be fair." Randy groaned a little about the pay raise, but I think he was expecting it. He did get defensive about Bobby. We should understand, he explained. Not all drug users are bad and he is under a lot of stress with a sick wife and 3 kids. I pointed out that those were more reasons not to put him in a position where it would be easier to slip back into old habits. We all agreed on the changes and Randy said he was going home to get some rest. After he left, we talked among ourselves, and we were all worried. What would this extra stress do to him? Pam was going to suggest a short day this Thursday. She was expecting a cancellation for a big afternoon case. The patient had not received medical clearance and was needing a further workup. She needed time with Randy to put these new ideas into place.

Thursday afternoon Claudia's nurse friend from the hospital came in to look at the office. She had worked recovery for years and we thought she would fit in well. Claudia being able to work between surgery and recovery was a big help. Pam set up an appointment with the bank president for her and Randy. Without disclosing too much information, they explained that the office computers had been hacked and they wanted to limit the data available online. She emphasized that this was temporary until the hacker could be caught. The banker was happy to help a high-volume client any way she could. She set up a separate account for patient deposits and suggested using a prepaid phone for running credit card purchases. Pam would keep all of these records separate and use the old-style ledger. Randy hoped the hacker would see business falling off and give up the harassment. They came back from the bank feeling positive. At least something was being done. Pam called the accountant to make sure everything was being set up properly. He was sorry that we had to resort to such measures, but knew we had to preserve patient confidentiality.

When they got back to the office Randy called Buddy and decided to make it a big promotion and get as much publicity as possible out of it. They decided on a date and Buddy started really talking it up on his show. Randy offered a 2-area liposuction. The patient would pay for their pre-op medical clearance and for the post-op garment. I knew how much stress Randy was under, so I comped my anesthesia fee. Randy was hoping that whoever won would get a good result. Many people think you can get liposuction as a means of weight loss, but it isn't true. Patients are often advised to lose weight before getting liposuction. It works best when it is done to improve problem areas. There had been a lot of publicity during the newspaper expose' regarding liposuction. Some patients were having liposuction to remove large amounts of fat along with tummy tucks or other large procedures, and there had been some major problems, including fatalities. The state medical board rules limited the amount of fat that could be removed at one time and what procedures could be done at the same time. Randy had always been more conservative, so the new rules did not affect our policies very much. His larger patients would come back for a second procedure and sometimes follow with loose skin excisions. He liked to see the results from the first liposuction with all the swelling gone, and then decide what was needed.

The radio contest winner turned out to be a great candidate. Buddy came to the office and broadcast again from the pre-op room. One contest rule was the winner had to agree to be interviewed and speak openly about her experience. She was very pleased and it turned out to be good advertising. Randy got more calls and bookings from this contest than he did from

Buddy's live procedure. The radio station was pleased too and Buddy suggested they do it annually. Randy laughed and agreed, but inside he wondered if he would even be here in another year.

Chapter 24

Pam hired an assistant and she really needed it. The extra work of keeping separate accounts was time-consuming. She was very organized and this was much more work. There had been no activity from the internet troll for a few weeks, but she knew better than to relax.

The next blow to Randy and his practice did not come from the internet. The office was very busy. We were doing surgery 4 days a week with only one day for patient consults. Pam said she thought we were losing patients because they had to wait too long for an appointment. Randy said to bring a few consults in between surgical cases a couple of days a week, but Teri didn't like it. She was busy with the surgical patient and couldn't always be with Randy in the consult room. Pam would go in her place, but she was not a nurse and sometimes busy too. All male doctors are aware that you must have a female staff member present in the room when a female patient is examined. It is usually okay if the patient has a male significant other with her, but it is still always best to have a female staff member there. One busy day there was a consult scheduled between the second and third cases. It was one of our previous patients who told Pam she was bringing her cousin in for a consult. She was so happy with her breast surgery that her cousin wanted it too. Pam told her it could run a little late because it was between cases. She said they were in no hurry and she would be with her cousin.

The day was crazy and when they arrived Pam put them both in a consult room. Teri was still in the OR with me and our surgery patient and Pam had a line of people at the desk. Randy had finished in the OR and walked into the consulting room. He recognized the patient from her previous surgery and she introduced him to her cousin. He went ahead and did the breast consult and exam. It was very congenial and after he went to the kitchen to grab some lunch. Teri came in upset. "Did you see that consult by yourself?" Teri asked. "No". Randy replied. "Her cousin was in the room. She is our patient. She even took her shirt off to show her cousin. She is very pleased with her surgery." "Please, Randy, don't do that again. It makes me nervous that you didn't have a staff member there. Also, I need this time to get a rapport going with the patient." "You're right, Teri. I won't do it again."

About 2 weeks later Randy was seeing patients. When he came out of the room Pam was waiting for him with steam coming from her head and daggers coming from her eyes. "Come to your office. Right now." She marched ahead of him and was obviously very angry. "Look at this". She flung a letter at him. It was from a lawyer who was writing on behalf of his 2 clients. They were the previous patient and her cousin. They were accusing Randy of being abusive and sexually harassing them. They said he had demanded that the patient show her previous breast surgery and had then fondled both of them. Then he unzipped his pants and stroked himself. They said they were traumatized and were both getting counseling. They didn't want to press charges, but felt they needed compensation for counseling services and for their mental suffering. They wanted $40000. It was extortion, plain and simple. Randy could not believe it. "She was a happy patient. Why would she do this?" he asked. Pam said "Because they saw an opportunity. You don't know your patients, Randy. You see them for a short time through a procedure. They could be professional con women. You don't know. All I know is that you didn't follow your own office policy, and this is going to cost you." Randy was defensive. "I didn't do anything. I will deny everything. It's my word against them." "Exactly", Pam said as she paced around the room. "The first thing their lawyer will ask is why you didn't have a staff member in the room. Then he will imply that you wanted it that way because they are young and attractive. Do you want to go to court and have all of this in the newspaper and on local news? Social media will go crazy. I'm going to call your attorney and have him come here as soon as possible. This letter is giving you one week to respond or they are going to file charges." Randy was completely dejected and slumped into his chair. Everything had been quiet on the internet since the radio contest. He actually had caught a breath and was hoping maybe his stalker was backing off. And now this. I am not a naïve person, he thought. How could I not see what they were doing? It seemed like a normal consult with nothing unusual. Pam came back and told him the lawyer was coming at 4:30.

Patients were gone, so Teri, Pam and Randy met with the lawyer in the kitchen. He shook his head and was not encouraging. "I think Pam is right, Randy. It looks like these girls are probably familiar with scams and saw an opportunity. If it truly happened as they say it did, they would have gone immediately to the police and pressed charges. Instead, you get a letter 2 weeks later. I don't think they planned it originally, and that's why it seemed so normal to you, Randy. After they left, they started kicking around the idea. I know this lawyer's name. He hangs around the jails and courts looking for clients and was almost disbarred once. I hate to say this, but in your position, I think you should pay them off. Randy was angry. "This is extortion. I'm being hounded by an internet stalker and now this. What happens if I don't pay? Maybe we can dig up dirt on these 2 women. They could have records for doing this to other people." The lawyer put away his papers and closed his briefcase. He looked at Randy with sympathetic eyes. "You are right, Randy. We could do all of those things, but a lot of people think that where there is smoke, there is fire. When there are allegations of sexual misconduct, you will lose a lot of patients. They could post terrible things about you online. They could picket your office and carry signs saying Pervert. No one knows what these 2 will do. I do know that you have a lot more to lose than either of them. We can offer them a small settlement, and I will demand a nondisclosure letter, so they can't come back again. I'll figure something out." "What kind of money are you looking at?" Randy asked. "Let me mull this over and I'll get back to you tomorrow. The sooner we shut this down, the better." The lawyer left everyone sitting in disbelief. Pam was still incensed. "Randy, those leeches dreamed this up after they left the office. One knew our routine and she saw a break. The other bitch just wants enough to pay for a breast augmentation. No more of these insane days, and no more consults on surgery days. I can't stand it." She stormed out of the room and left for the day. Teri looked at Randy. "I'm sorry, Doc," she said. "I wish I had been there". "It's not your fault, Teri. It's mine. I was overconfident because she had been a patient and I am pushing a busy schedule. This internet hacker has put such pressure on me that I'm not thinking things through. All of you are the best staff anyone could ask for. Thanks for your support." Teri left too. Randy pulled a small bottle of his favorite scotch out of his drawer and poured a healthy drink. He heard the back door open and saw Wes Ford coming down the hall to do the terminal cleaning. "Hey Doc, how are you? I haven't seen you in a while." "Have a seat for a minute, Wes. You want a little scotch?" Wes laughed. "No thanks. Sounds good, but then I won't want to do my cleaning. You look a little down. Is everything OK?" Randy looked pensive." I don't know, Wes. I worked my ass off for a long time to get here and now I wonder if it was even worth it. I have always loved being a surgeon, but it's beating me down. I wonder if I will ever feel happy again." Wes looked sympathetic. "You just started out in this office a couple of years ago and you are one of the main men right now. After you get more financially secure, you could take a sabbatical for a while. Go on the Mercy ship or Doctors Without Borders for a few months and let your talent and brains change people's lives. You will meet many people that need you and maybe you need them. It's something for your future." Randy finished his drink and shook Wes' hand. "Wes, I think you are on to something. That is a goal I could aspire to. Thanks, Buddy."

The next day the lawyer came by between cases, and brought a draft of the letter. He offered $10,000 for their inconvenience and had a letter of nondisclosure to be signed by all parties. He stated Randy's innocence and inferred this could be construed as extortion. He said he was sure they would turn it down. "They are probably splitting it 3 ways," he said. "I think he will counter with $30000, and we will counter back with $15000. I will tell them it's a final offer. They may turn it down and come back with $20000, but we stay firm. I will tell them we have talked to a detective and he is encouraging us to press charges for extortion and blackmail. We stay firm at $15000 and I think they will take it. They will get $5000 each. I think it was a spur-of-the-moment thing, and they won't get too greedy. What do you think?" Pam was still pissed. "I don't want to give them a dime," she said. Randy agreed. "I don't either, but I want this gone. Go ahead and send the letter".

Randy did well through this latest stress. He had been taking Adderall on surgery days and he felt confident taking it. He thought it had helped him to focus and not dwell on his worries, but he still had trouble sleeping. He found that he did best when he had a couple of drinks after work and took Xanax for sleep. He was feeling very isolated though. He saw his kids on the weekend and that was about it. He was working all the time. He decided to call Mitch and suggest dinner on Friday night. Mitch had a great social life, dated beautiful women and knew some fun places to go. He needed to get out and have a good time, so they made plans for a guy's night out.

Chapter 25

Randy woke up Saturday morning with a start. It was almost 10 a.m. Wow, he thought, I haven't slept this late in years. He had to smile as he thought of how much fun he had last night. Mitch took him to a new restaurant in Winter Park and then to a club downtown. He thought the downtown clubs were all for the younger crowd, but Mitch knew where to go. His ego was polished when several women came on to him. One gorgeous brunette CPA invited him back to her house and he was really tempted. Getting involved with anyone now did not seem like a good idea. He wasn't actually divorced and the stress and worry he was going through was sometimes overwhelming. He kept her number and maybe he would call her in the future. He had been dragging yesterday afternoon and had taken an extra Adderall. He had perked up and had a great time. He decided he would take a second one every afternoon to avoid the afternoon slump. He had taken Xanax last night and with the alcohol he had at the club, he slept like a log and felt great today. He was spending the weekend with his kids and looking forward to it. Before he got in the shower, he called his wife and told her he was taking the kids to Sea World. While in the shower he decided to get a hotel room near there. It would be a treat for the kids and he would make it a fun weekend. He was proud of himself too. He had been approached at the club by people offering him cocaine, pot, meth, or whatever he wanted. He turned it all down. He was feeling okay with the Adderall, alcohol, and Xanax. He was confident that he was in control and soon would get away from the stress.

The lawyer came back the next week with a response from the con girl's lawyer. They countered with $25000. He prepared a new letter staying at the $15000 offer. He also said that he was prepared to go to the police and file charges of blackmail and extortion. He also mentioned that Randy had many friends in the media who would challenge their phony charges. He was very terse and said this was the final offer. Randy looked it over and told him to send it. The lawyer felt confident that they would take it. Less than a week later, he was right. Randy was seething when he had to write the check, but he wanted it over with. Business was very good. We were doing 15 cases this week and Pam was scheduling weeks in advance. There had been nothing from the internet hacker for a couple of months. We were hoping he had lost interest and moved on, but that was not the case.

A couple of weeks had passed since the settlement with the con girls. Randy had started out in a great mood but had become grumpier as the week went on. He complained that he wasn't sleeping. He seemed okay in the mornings and then got a second wind in the afternoons. Many days we didn't finish until after 7 pm. We were all tired and asked about cutting back a bit, but he just pushed harder. He wanted to fill every minute of the day, but we knew he was tired too. One day I noticed that his hands were shaky at the end of the day. I tried to talk to him about it, but he just walked off in a huff. He slammed the door to his office and sat down at his desk. He looked at his hands and there was a tremor. He poured some scotch and gulped it down. He started to relax and he looked at his hands again. They were better. Maybe I am working too hard, he thought. I will tell Pam to get us a lighter week. I don't want to burn out the staff. He went to check on the patient before he left and saw me looking through charts for the patients tomorrow. "I'm sorry, Sunny. I was really short with you". I decided to be honest. "Randy, we all think you are doing too much. You haven't been yourself and you aren't sleeping. Can't we slow down a little? You haven't been here 3 years. You have lots of time to grow your business." He thought about his long-term goals. "I know, Sunny. But life is uncertain. Look at all the crazy crap that has happened. I'm going to tell Pam to see if she can get us a little break, but we have to be aware that work can dry up quickly. The economy or some political decision can have an effect on business. We have to do the work while we have it. Hang in with me and I'm sure things will eventually settle down."

It had been almost 3 months since Charlie had made any contact with Randy or the office. He had been preoccupied. One day he ordered takeout from one of his favorite Italian restaurants. As he was standing in line to pick up his order, he couldn't help but notice the lovely perfume scent lightly emanating from the woman in front of him. She smiled at him and made a couple of casual friendly comments. Their orders came out at the same time and they both laughed because they had ordered the same thing. They chatted as they walked out to their cars and Charlie asked if she was eating alone. She said she was. He said he was too and suggested they meet the next week for dinner inside. There were smiles and an exchange of phone numbers. That was the start of a fun friendship that was turning into much more. His life had been lonely and empty for a long time. The knowledge of what happened to Laura had really thrown him. He had to decide what to do about Randy. Should he just leave it alone and not contact him again? He hoped he had inflicted some pain and fear in his life. He had noticed that there was a change in the financials in the office and he could tell money was being diverted to other accounts. That was probably a suggestion from his lawyer or accountant. The money that Randy had paid out was nothing compared to what he was he was earning. He would come up with one more scheme to antagonize him and then he would shut it down. He would wipe all the computers clean and walk away. He knew he had not affected Randy's success. He was still very busy and one of the top plastic surgeons in Orlando. But he knew Randy's personality, and he was sure there was fear, anxiety and he was waiting for the next shoe to drop. That was all he wanted, and it was for Laura. His final plan would not involve money. Something a little more frightening was in order for his finale.

Chapter 26

We had a terrible Friday. Pam tried to keep Fridays scheduled light, but this was not one of them. We had 2 extra patients that we had to squeeze into our already busy day. Both were revision patients and Randy was annoyed that we had to redo the surgery. Since he started his practice, we had very few surgical revisions. He was always very meticulous and if something wasn't the best, he worked at it until it was. Because our schedule was so full recently, he was letting little things slide. One patient needed a breast revision. She was unhappy because one breast was lower than the other. I remembered the day of her original surgery. He contemplated removing the implant and adjusting the pocket, but decided not to do it. Of course, she complained and she was justified. The other patient was a liposuction. In order to get a nice hip line, we needed to turn the patient on her side. Turning patients has to be done carefully and it adds time to the procedure. He said he could do it without turning, but it wasn't as good as it could have been. She was also correct in being unhappy. Both cases took longer than expected on top of our already full day. He was mad at himself for not taking more time during the original surgery, and this made him even more irritable. We took a little break around 4:00 and he came back energized. In our last case, I noticed his hands were shaky again and he was having trouble suturing. I suggested that we stop for a bit and he take a break. He got very angry and blamed his suturing problem on Becky. "Your damn hands are in the way and you are blocking the light" he yelled at her. He finished suturing and threw the instruments on the OR table. "What I need is staff that knows what the fuck they are doing" he screamed and stormed out. Teri, Becky, and I just looked at each other. "What the hell was that all about?" Teri asked. Becky said "This closure sucks. I'm going to fix a few of these stitches." Becky had been a scrub nurse for many years and could close skin better than a lot of surgeons. Pam came back and asked what was happening. He loudly slammed the door to his office, she said, and there were family members in the waiting room. "I told them there was a problem with the door and we were getting a repairman in to fix it. What the hell is going on?"

I got the patient settled in the recovery room and was going back to clean up my anesthesia cart when Randy called me into his office. "I want you to talk to the patient's family. Tell them everything went fine and I had to go to the hospital for an emergency". "Randy, what is wrong? This is not like you at all. You have been off all day." He glared at me. "Don't you start in. Just do what I asked. I need people around that support me, not sit around judging me." He gulped down whatever was in a glass on his desk and started getting ready to leave. "Randy, no one judges you. We all love you and are worried. You have never acted like this. What can we do to help you?" "All of you can get off of my fucking back. That's what you can do. Now go talk to the families like I asked." He picked up his briefcase and walked out the back entrance. I was in shock and did not know this man. I checked the 2 patients who were still in recovery and spoke cheerfully to their families. I apologized that Randy was not able to see them and explained that he had an emergency call. After the patients were gone, Pam made coffee and we all sat in the kitchen. "I know he's drinking," Pam said. Becky was skeptical. "I think it's more than that. I have lived with alcoholics and this is different. Did you see his hands shaking on the last case?"

Teri looked at me. "Why don't you ask Mitch if he has any idea what is going on with him. He sees him pretty often". "I will", I said, "but I don't like this. He never leaves when there is a patient in recovery. She was barely awake. And he always likes to talk to the patient's family. This is not his standard of care. The other thing bothering me is why he gets this big lift in the middle of the afternoon. We are all wearing down and he's energized. That's been going on for a while and it all really bothers me." Pam said she was going to look for any way she could lessen the load next week. We were all upset with his behavior, but more than anything, we were worried about him.

Two cases were canceled the next week and Pam didn't fill the spots. That would give him a break, so he could go home a little earlier. Instead, he had a fit and reamed Pam for not filling the time. "I want every bit of time filled" he shouted at Pam. All week he was agitated and complaining about everything. He said he went to the hospital surgical staff meeting and was sure that someone there was behind the internet hacking. The other plastic surgeons were jealous and hated him, so he was going to quit going to the meetings. The hospital always did a very nice dinner for the medical staff and everyone enjoyed it. He said it looked terrible and he wasn't hungry, so he didn't eat. Friday was the worst day. Our third patient was a breast augmentation and she had breast swelling in the recovery room. Claudia dreaded telling him that it looked like a hematoma, which is internal bleeding, and a trip back to surgery to explore inside and control the bleeding. We took her back to surgery and opened the breast. There were clots everywhere. He removed the implant, irrigated the breast pocket, and searched for the bleeder. He packed the breast with cold sponges and held pressure for a while to get the bleeding under control. Visibility was better and he was able to find the bleeding vessel. He bitched the entire time because it was everyone else's fault. Becky didn't sponge properly and blocked his vision. Teri and I were too rough taking her to the recovery room. Claudia let her move too much. We were all against him. If we didn't start doing better, he was going to clean house. No one said anything, but we all thought the same thing. If he had not been in such a hurry, he would have found the bleeder during the original procedure and this would not have happened.

We finally finished the last case and he stormed out. We were all quiet, and Becky said she wanted to talk to us after cleaning up. Pam made coffee while I finished paperwork and Teri discharged the patient. We all sat in the kitchen and Becky said "I'm giving my 2-week notice. I'm going back to the hospital." We were all very upset and told Becky we could understand why she felt that way, but begged her to reconsider. She was really important to the practice and we needed her. She cried a little, but she had made up her mind. "I have been thinking about this for a while. I loved Randy and loved working here, but he has changed. I have stress at home and I don't need it here too. We are all walking on eggshells because we don't know when he is going to blow up. Even worse is the fact that he takes no responsibility for his own actions. I know he has been under a lot of pressure, but that isn't our fault. I just want to go to work, do a good job, and go home. I know he is drinking and he might be doing something else. He is getting sloppy in his work and I don't want to be part of any of it. He pays very well and you will get someone else. I love you guys, but I can't deal with him anymore. I know Pat from the hospital would jump at this job. She is sick of call and the salary is really good. She doesn't take any guff from the surgeons and she can handle Randy. " By now we were all crying and Pam asked her to just try it a little longer. "Please give it one more week" Pam begged. "I'm going to talk to him. Just a week-for us." Becky reluctantly agreed. "OK. One more week," she said. "But if I were you, I would talk to Pat and see if she is interested. It is still part of my notice." She left and the 3 of us sat looking at each other. "I'm going to talk to him Monday morning," Pam said. "I don't know if it will do any good, but I have to try. I know he really likes Becky and this is not like him." "Sunny, will you talk to Mitch and see if he was at the staff meeting or has seen Randy lately? Maybe he has some insight."

I called Mitch to ask if he had seen Randy. He asked if I had plans. I did not, so he said he would pick up pizza and stop by. I made a drink and poured a beer for him. We opened the pizza and went out on the lanai. "He came to the staff meeting," he said. "He wasn't himself. He sat next to me and went on and on about how the medical staff here were all out to get him. They were jealous of his success. He thought a couple of them might have pooled money and hired an internet hacker to destroy his practice. There were a couple of people looking at him because he was loud, and then he said everyone was staring at him. It was real paranoia. I tried to calm him down, but he just wouldn't keep quiet. They had a great dinner, as usual, but he wouldn't eat. He said the quality of food had gone downhill and he wasn't hungry. I could smell alcohol on him at the meeting, but he wasn't drunk. Then he just left. If no one was talking about him before, they probably are now." I hated to hear it. I told him about the hematoma and how he had reacted. "It hasn't been that long ago that he had the hematoma on the facelift guy who went out for steak," he said. "That was totally the patient's fault. It was a mess, but he was in complete control. I think this whole internet thing is driving him over the edge. What do you think, Sunny?" I cleaned up from the pizza and made us each a fresh drink. "I think he is using some kind of upper. It could be cocaine or some kind of amphetamine. He comes in energetic in the morning and then winds down. By 2 or 3 he's revitalized and then a little later he gets shaky. The other thing is his personality change. He's always angry or agitated and he is treating the staff poorly. Becky gave a 2-week notice today and Pam talked her into hanging in for an extra week. I'll bet she leaves. Pam said she is going to try to talk to Randy on Monday, but I don't know if it will help." "I hate to hear that," said Mitch. "That is a big loss. Becky is a great tech. She really knows plastic surgery and she is a loyal worker." We talked for a long time and ended up with no ideas for what to do.

Chapter 27

Randy did not have a good day either. He was agitated and anxious. He thought about the hematoma patient. Becky kept getting in the way of the light and that was why he missed the bleeder. Or maybe Sunny and Teri were too rough moving her. Claudia could have let her thrash around. The patient might have taken aspirin and hadn't told them. He paced around his kitchen and thought about eating something. He had to tighten his belt again this morning because he had lost more weight. He just wasn't hungry and he could not relax. He poured some scotch and washed down a Xanax. They were not working as well as they had before and taking it with scotch seemed to help. Maybe he needed something besides Xanax. He had tried Klonopin and a couple of others, but they weren't any better. He just needed to find the right combination. The afternoon Adderall really improved his stamina for the later cases, but sleeping was a big problem. He was finally starting to relax a little. He turned on the History Channel sipped more scotch and took another Xanax. He was hoping he would doze off and get a good long sleep. He had been getting 3-4 hours a night for weeks and was feeling it. He did doze off, but woke up around 1 a.m. He went right to bed, but could not fall asleep. He tossed and turned until around 4 and gave up. He got up and went back to the TV. He would drift in and out and by 7 he gave up and took a shower. He had promised to take the kids to lunch and a movie, so he had to get with it. He ate a little breakfast and took an Adderall. He was really tired and hopefully, it would get him going. He thought about the hematoma patient again. Maybe he didn't take enough time exploring the pocket before he put in the implant or maybe he was hurrying too much. He could have missed the bleeder. Pam always gave him a list of each day's surgical patients and their phone numbers. He found his lab coat and checked the pocket. There was the list. He called the patient's home and spoke to her husband. He asked how she was doing and spoke to her explaining that she would be really bruised for a while. They were both very pleased that he had called them. When he hung up, it came to mind that he used to call every patient the night of surgery. He had not done that in a while. I need to do a reset of my life, he thought. It is all of this stress I have been dealing with. I'm going to work as hard as I can for the next year and then I am leaving this rat race. Circumstances that I cannot change or understand are controlling my life. I will get back on track by finding the right combination of meds to help me do it. He could feel his energy coming back. He would pick up the kids early and take them to the park. He needed to get some exercise.

He had a good day with the kids and was really tired when he got home. He read a couple of medical journals, hoping that would make him sleepy, but no luck. He was feeling very anxious and craved some sleep. I shouldn't have taken that second Adderall, he thought, but then he would have been dragging with the kids. I need to find something better for sleep. That is the answer. If I could get a good night's sleep, I know I could make it fine. He gulped down a second Xanax with some scotch and shortly after drifted off to sleep. I will figure this out tomorrow. I only have to do this for another year.

The week started out normally. Randy was in a better mood and a little more like himself. Pam and

I were crossing our fingers that Becky would decide to stay. He saw consults on Wednesday and the schedule was filling up. Thursday and Friday were very tense. He looked tired when he came in and by the afternoon cases, he was very shaky. He had to redo 2 closures because they looked terrible. He picked at Becky all day Friday and we knew that was her last straw. He accused each one of us of being responsible for his poor performance. He stormed out with 2 patients still in Recovery. One patient had a partial skin separation on the closure and it was oozing a bit. Becky did a few more stitches and it looked much better. When she finished, she came to Pam's office and said she was done. She could not work under these conditions and she had lost faith in the quality of Randy's work. She would work with Pat next week, but only until Wednesday. That was her last day. We knew it was coming, but we all felt terrible. Teri said she needed to speak to Pam and me. "I don't know what to make of this, but I'm really concerned. Randy took me aside between cases and told me he had accidentally broken a vial of Fentanyl. He said he was looking for something for a headache in the narcotic box and the box of Fentanyl fell on the counter. One vial was broken. He knows that 2 people are supposed to witness disposal, but said he had forgotten and thrown it away in the red box. He initialed the narcotic sheet, but I don't like this. He has never done anything like it before. The red box was over half full, so I could not tell if it was in there. The office key to the narcotic box is not in its usual place. I asked him where he put it and he didn't answer me. What do you both think?" I spoke up immediately. "I am really concerned with what is going on with him. He is erratic, angry, unreasonable, and getting scary. I am going to talk to Mitch about how to proceed with an intervention. He is going to hurt someone. Teri, just keep the day's narcotic needs in the regular box. Pam put the extra drugs in a separate small locked box and put that in the safe. Keep a close eye on all of it. If he is using narcotics, it's a game changer. We will have to do something drastic." I called Mitch and asked if I could see him over the weekend. He had a date that night, but we planned dinner for Saturday night. I left feeling sick inside. He was going from bad to worse.

Randy was very agitated when he left. Why can't my staff just do what I need them to do? I think they want me to look bad. He took the vial of Fentanyl out of his pocket and looked at it. I think this is the answer, he thought. I will only use a tiny bit at night. No scotch. That will get me the sleep I need. Between that and Xanax, it will calm my anxiety too. If I can sleep, I can make it through the hard days and it's only temporary. Once I get my life under control, I will think about going back to rehab. Life was great when I left rehab, and I felt energetic and in control. Since that damn hacker came along, everything has gone to hell. He had some scotch and thought about the evening ahead. Maybe he would go to the club that Mitch had taken him to. He had fun and that sounded really good right now. He showered and dressed up but felt a bit tired, so he took another Adderall. Then he wondered if he had taken one or two earlier in the afternoon, but he couldn't remember. He felt energized and went to the club. He danced and was getting attention from several women. After a couple of drinks, he noticed that some of the men were staring at him. They are probably jealous, he thought. He looked around and almost everyone was looking at him. He noticed 2 men sitting in a corner speaking very quietly. I think they are talking about me or maybe they are after me, he thought. I wonder if the hacker is here now. He could be following me, just waiting for a chance to do something. He was really getting anxious and decided to leave. He drove home, but there were people walking nearby. Why are they here, he thought. They may be casing my house, so he drove away and decided to get a drink at a small pub nearby. He had so much on his mind it was hard to focus. Could his staff be behind the hacking? It had led to them getting raises. He could fire them all and get new people. Maybe he should get rid of the big facility and just do surgery in the outpatient department. It would be a lot easier to manage and that's what Mitch did. Maybe Mitch was behind the hacking. He is probably jealous of me too. Or I could just walk away from the whole thing. I have a lot of money put away and I could go somewhere else and start over. The thoughts were running through his head like wildfire. He decided that a drive might be relaxing. He felt very tense and noticed that the bartender was giving him odd looks. He didn't feel like going home and he wasn't tired. How much Adderall had he taken today? He wasn't sure. Three, four or maybe more, but it didn't matter. Then he noticed a man who had been in the pub walking toward his car. Is he going to come at me? He started his car quickly and drove out of the lot. In his mirror he saw the man driving behind him. He's following me, he thought. He made several turns and pulled behind a closed strip mall until he was sure the man was gone. What was that voice he heard? Had someone called his name? Three young men were walking through the parking lot. They looked suspicious. Were they going to rob him? He quickly drove away and was sure the men were pointing and laughing at him. Relief flooded over him when he could no longer see them. That was a close call, he thought. He drove aimlessly and soon found he was near the airport. There were directional signs to the coast. The beach is where he would go. He loved the beach and it was always relaxing. He drove due east for 30 minutes and across the causeway to the beach in Indialantic. It was after 4 a.m. Why was it so late? He parked in a public spot, opened the windows, and listened to the hypnotic song of crashing waves. Maybe I should move here. I could still see the kids and the staff could commute. His earlier fears started sneaking back in and he was determined to push them away when he saw a swirling blue light behind him. A cop. What have I done? They may plant something on me and then arrest me. I have to be very careful. An officer came to the passenger window and shined his flashlight inside. "Good evening, Sir," he said. "Is everything OK?" "Yes, Officer. I am a plastic surgeon and was having trouble sleeping, so I drove down here to relax and listen to the waves. I was just getting ready to go home and try sleeping again." "May I see your license and registration?" Randy was very composed and professional. "Certainly. I have it right here." The officer took it back to his car and ran the info. I wonder if he is going to accuse me of some crap and arrest me, he thought. He turned on his cell phone so he could record any conversation in case he might need evidence. The officer returned his documents. "You have a long drive home, Dr. Are you sure you are OK to drive? If you are tired, there are a lot of hotels in the area." "Thanks, Officer. I'm fine. I had a busy week and some tough cases. I just needed to relax. I'm going home now." "Drive safely," the officer said as he walked away. Whew, that's a relief he thought. Why did that cop suggest a hotel? He probably knows the place and who knows what he would have done. He might have come there later and beaten me. It was almost time for sunrise and he would have liked to see it, but was afraid to stay any longer. He drove home slowly and thought about how lucky he was to have avoided confrontation with so many people.

When he got home, he showered and had coffee and toast. It dawned on him that he had not eaten since breakfast yesterday. While buttering a second piece of toast, he glanced at the calendar on the refrigerator. His son had an early game today. Damn. There would be no rest now. He took another Adderall and headed to the game. It started out fun, but he became more and more agitated. The other team was trying to make his son look bad. Even his son's teammates were not helping him. He yelled to his son to get more aggressive and soon he was shouting and calling the other boys names. The coach came over and asked him to please calm down. Name-calling was not allowed. "Doc, you are not yourself today. These are kids and we have rules of behavior. Are you OK?" He started berating the coach and called him a pussy. Then he stormed off toward his car.

His wife was there and followed him. "Randy, what is going on? You never act like this. Why are you so upset?" He turned on her and called her a spendthrift, a lousy mother and a pathetic wife. "All of this is your fault," he said as he jumped in his car and drove away. She was dumbfounded as she walked to her crying son. He must be having some kind of nervous breakdown, she worried.

Typical, he thought. All of them. Whiny ass weaklings. That stupid pussy coach is why they don't win more games. And that wife of his. If she had been the kind of woman I deserved, she wouldn't be on her way out.

He had been tugging at his pants all day because his belt could not hold them up. With the recent weight loss, his clothes hung on him. Being well-dressed had always been important to him, so he popped another Adderall and headed to the Millenia Mall where he went on a real shopping spree at several high-end stores. It was great fun because all of the salespeople catered to his every whim. His car was packed full of boxes of every size with sport coats, pants, shirts, belts and workout clothes. As he was driving away, he noticed one of the luxury jewelry stores and decided it was time for something special. He had been wanting a Rolex. They provided very individualized attention, which made him happy. He took everything home and laid it out all over the bedroom and living room. This is great, he thought. This is what I deserve. He made a sandwich but only ate a few bites. He wasn't really tired but thought he might get tired, so he had another Adderall. Now, where was he going to go tonight? He ended up driving around aimlessly all night. He just couldn't decide what to do and knew he could not sleep.

Mitch arrived at my house around 5 p.m. He came early, so we could talk before going to dinner. I made us a drink and updated him on the last few days. "Mitch, can we do an intervention? Can we force him to get some help? His taking a vial of Fentanyl is frightening. We don't know where to turn. What do you think?" Mitch looked very concerned. "It is not easy to get someone help that doesn't want it. We could hire an interventionist who could put it together. However, Randy would probably tell us all to get the hell out and call the police. He does not have to accept our suggestions. I wouldn't be surprised if that is what he would do."

"What about reporting him to the medical board? His work is getting worse every week." "Sunny, you have to have evidence. Have patients filed complaints? Have there been lawsuits? Have patients gone to other doctors to get his work revised? I don't think so. Has anyone seen him using any drugs? Does he have needle marks on his arms? Do you see what I am saying? There is no proof that he is doing anything illegal. Suspicions and surmises are not evidence. He could claim that he's been off kilter because of the stress of the internet hacker." "Mitch, I don't want to see someone harmed. Does a person have to die or be maimed before anyone pays attention? We know he is not in control. Can the Board of Medicine insist on a blood test or something to prove he is competent?" "There are no patient complaints. You can file a complaint to the Board that he may be working impaired. Guess what happens. Nothing. He has not beaten anyone up or been arrested. You do not have proof. His practice is filled with people who love their surgery and tell their friends. He has close associates on the Board, and believe me, they will protect him unless there is proof. You would be viewed as some sour grapes former employee. He has stayed out of trouble because he has a wonderful staff looking out for his patients and he basically is a good surgeon. I know it is scary and I worry too that someone is going to get hurt. However, the law is clear. You must have evidence and we have only conjecture. I will try again to talk to him and mention his erratic behavior. I will also suggest rehab, but I won't be surprised if he throws me out. He certainly is not open to any suggestions. Come on and let's go to dinner. I feel bad about Becky. She is a major loss."

We went to dinner and I mulled over what he said. He was right. Unfortunately, it usually takes some kind of extreme event to demand accountability. People later will say "We saw it coming, but there was nothing we could do." I started thinking about myself. I had always felt that I was a patient advocate and could help keep them safe. However, I did not know if I could continue in a situation that could lead to harm coming to someone. All of us felt completely helpless.

Chapter 28

Charlie Devon looked around his crowded kitchen. There were boxes everywhere and it was an exciting time. He was getting married in a couple of weeks and had accepted a job with an international cybersecurity firm in London. His fiancé had found a lovely flat to rent in a great part of the city and the company was giving him a generous moving package. He was giving most of his household goods away and they were taking just personal items. He headed to the basement to create his final bit of mayhem for Randy. His office was not the smooth-running machine it used to be. He hoped he had created some fear and uncertainty in that cocky exterior he was sure that Randy still possessed. He had disassembled most of his computer equipment, and when he finished with his final post to Randy's office, he would wipe the rest of it clean. It was all being donated to a local group that mentored middle schoolers. He looked at Laura's diary sitting on the desk. He hadn't decided if he would tell Randy the truth or

let him live in the uncertainty of another possible
hack. He would have to think about it.

Chapter 29

Sunday was a crazy day for Randy. He tried packing up most of his current clothes to donate. He had lost so much weight that nothing fit. He wanted to organize his closet with all the new things, but it was all too confusing. He kept mixing up the old with the new. He had dozed off for a couple of hours last night but kept waking up. Most of his Adderall was gone and he could not remember how much he had taken. He ate a bagel and wandered around making lists of all the things he needed to do. I need to focus, he thought, but decided against another Adderall. He felt too strung out. He noticed his hands were very shaky and knew he could not do surgery like this. If I got a really good night's sleep, I would be fine. He thought about the office and wondered what the staff was saying about him. By 6 p.m. he knew he had to do something to sleep. The anxiety was overwhelming. He found the vial of Fentanyl and went online and confirmed the usual dosage. He was familiar with it, but had never prescribed or used it for his patients. The anesthesia department always took care of Fentanyl or other anesthesia narcotics during the case and in the recovery room.

He would use just a tiny bit. Doing it IV was scary, but he was desperate for sleep and really thought it would be just what he needed. He had a small syringe with a tiny #30 needle and he drew up just a small amount. He had not used any alcohol or taken any Xanax today, so he would see if it helped. After injecting he held pressure on his vein and stretched out in his chair. He could feel the anxiety calming and he was so exhausted that he fell asleep. He woke up around 10 p.m. and was disoriented for a couple of minutes. He felt better and craved more delicious sleep. He took a Xanax and fell into the deepest sleep he had in weeks. When he awoke in the morning he felt like his old self. Rested and ready to go. That's it, he thought. I knew I just needed to find the right combination of drugs and I could get through this stress. When this is over, I can go to rehab or maybe just quit everything on my own. Now I know I can make it.

When he arrived at the office in the morning, Pam and Claudia were waiting for him. They were both very upset. "What's wrong?" he asked. Pam called him over to her computer and showed him her social media page. There were 2 photos of Claudia. A few months ago, she had a blepharoplasty, which is the removal of loose skin and fat pads on the upper and lower eyelids. Online were her before and after photos. Most of the patient photos were stored offline, but not all of them. They were supposedly posted by the office with a cheery message about how great she looked and how happy she was with the result. That was true, but no one from the office had posted it. Her records and photos had been hacked. Thankfully, no other patients were mentioned. They had been using a respected private server for recent record storage and had no issues, but the implication was clear. None of their records were safe. Pam said, "Randy, did you get any threats or emails telling you this was going to happen?" He admitted that he had not turned his computer on all weekend. He immediately went to his office and pulled up his email. There was one from "Your Friend". He called Pam in to see if she could get a photo of it before it disappeared once he opened it. All it said was "Don't forget who is in control." It disappeared immediately, but Pam did get a shot of it. "I'm calling Dalton," she said. "Maybe he can trace something through the social media account". "Close down the account," Randy said. "We can't take a chance that there could be others". He called Claudia in and told her he was sorry. She was a good sport about it. "It's ok, Doc. I would have allowed you to use them if you wanted to. It was quite a shock, though. I love my results and tell people all the time. Thank goodness it was me and not one of your regular patients".

Randy was pretty calm considering the morning shock. Pam came back and told us that Dalton had gotten the account immediately taken down and the website was looking at their security to see if we could get any info. He put a blocker on anyone attempting to reopen the account. She also told us that Pat would be coming in as soon as she could Monday and Tuesday to work with Becky for orientation. Wednesday was Becky's last day, and Randy told her that he was sorry she was leaving. It was the first time he acknowledged that she had resigned. Becky didn't want hard feelings, so she said it was because of her responsibilities at home. Randy was subdued all day. One of the afternoon cases was canceled, so Randy asked Pam to call his financial planner and see if he could squeeze him in for a meeting. She did that and also told us that Dalton had called back. The social media company took down the website, but could not find any useful information about the posting of the photos. It appeared that it came from our office. Randy left for his appointment and we were all glad for a light day. Pat came in and was surprised that we were finished with surgery. She was very pleasant and eager for the new job and Becky took her back to the OR to show her around. I left early and Claudia was leaving at the same time. "Are you OK, Claudia?" I asked. "That must have been quite a shock seeing yourself online". She laughed. "You're right, but I'm fine. He did my surgery for free and I would have let him use my pictures. It's scary though. I wonder if the person who hacked this knew I was an employee." I thought about it. "I'll bet they did and they probably know everything about this office. It was a threat. See what I can do, if I want to. I feel bad for Randy. Have you noticed how much weight he's lost?" She agreed and we left. I just wondered who could hate him so much to do this to him.

Randy went home after his meeting with the financial planner. The advice had been to keep up the work schedule. He was making a lot of money, and if he stayed at this pace, he would be in a very good position in a year. He would be well placed to either sell the practice or cut back to a comfortable schedule. He felt very down today. He was still exhausted and hoped he would sleep again tonight. He poured a scotch and caught up on paperwork. He had only taken one Adderall today and hoped that would help with sleep. He missed the afternoon bump that kept him going. He took a Xanax with a little more scotch and fell asleep for a few hours.

The rest of the week was a roller coaster. Randy started out convinced that the hacker was going to disclose other patient photos. He had Pam pull up all patient photos and put them on a separate flash drive so there were none stored on the office computer. Then he told her get them all professionally printed and put into books. No internet photos were available at all. It was a big job and Pam and her assistant were working extra. She had bought a new computer a few months ago and it was never connected to the internet, so she could put them there. She used it for schedules and other office info. It worked on a small scale, but there were so many patients by now that she was limited. She was going crazy with the extra work and inconvenience. Randy was convinced that the hacker was someone very close and was betraying him. Thursday he was a mess. He came late and upset the schedule. Then he complained all day because we were behind. He pushed and pushed and wanted us to skip lunch and dive into our third case. This was Pat's first day and she didn't want to set a precedent of not getting lunch. She said no. She had been running all day and she needed lunch and a little break. We all agreed and he stormed into his office to pout. He rushed through the last case and we had to call him back as he was leaving. Several sutures had come out and the closure was terrible. He had to redo it. He yelled at Pat that she should do it and said "You are perfectly capable of closing this. What am I paying you for?" She stared right at him and said "You are paying me to be a surgical assistant. The patient is paying you to close their surgical incision." She took no nonsense from him and we admired her. He muttered some more and finished the closure. I was really upset. Bleeding, hematomas, and wound openings were happening frequently. We had worked well over 2 years with only a rare complication. Now they were commonplace. His work was crap and his attitude was in the toilet. Tomorrow I would have it out with him. I complained to Pam and she felt the same. "I have been with him since he came to Orlando and this is not the same man. I am fearful for him, angry at him and worried about him all at the same time. I just don't know what to do" she said. "Pam, I am afraid that a patient is going to get hurt. I am confronting him tomorrow and I don't care if he fires me. He has to do something to get himself under control." I called Mitch on my way home and asked if I could stop by his office. He could tell I was upset and told me he would wait.

I filled him in about the recent complications we were seeing, and my fears for patient safety. He said "I didn't realize it was getting this bad. I've called him a couple of times, but he was busy. About a week ago he called me at 3:30 a.m. I thought maybe he needed help with an emergency. He just babbled and then hung up. I thought he was drinking. I called him back the next day, but he didn't answer." I told him that I intended to confront Randy tomorrow. "There has to be a way to get advice from the Board of Medicine," I said. "We can't wait until someone is injured". We discussed it for a while and Mitch said he was going to write a letter to both of Randy's friends that were on the Board. He would write personal letters and ask for their advice as a friend. They had likely dealt with this situation before and maybe would have some insight. He knew Randy would be furious, but he didn't care. "The person we are dealing with now is not the Randy that I have known for years. How do you think he will react to you?" I thought about it and said "I honestly don't know. He may fire me or I'm prepared to walk away, if necessary. I can't go on like this, Mitch." He suggested we go to dinner. "I have something else to talk to you about, and this would be a good time."

We went to a small local place and made small talk while we ordered drinks. "You know the Rozier Orthopedic Group?" he asked. "Sure. I always liked Dr. Rozier and all of the orthos in his group when I was at the hospital. Why?" "He asked me a few months ago if I would be interested in using his new surgical center. It is beautiful and top notch. It is near the hospital and I'm thinking about taking my patients there instead of the hospital outpatient department. He also asked me if you were happy working with Randy. He is very interested in hiring you for their center. I never mentioned it to you because I thought it would be disloyal to Randy, and I knew you were happy there. Now with you in this uncertain position, I felt you should know." That was a surprise. "If you are looking at it, there must be other specialties besides orthopedics," I said. He nodded. "They have 2 rooms set up for ortho and a third room for other cases. They would give me a regular day if I wanted it. They also have interest from other plastic and general surgeons. I know you are loyal, Sunny, but I understand what you are saying. We can all do whatever we can, but there comes a point where you have to look after yourself. Think about it and let me know what happens tomorrow with Randy."

Chapter 30

I felt very determined the next day. I was going to tell Randy the truth about his behavior and I hoped he would listen to me. We had all been loving and supportive, now was the time for hard facts. Hearing about the potential job offer had been good for my ego and I went in feeling positive. Randy was in a dark mood. He looked haggard and tired. We had 3 cases and were done by 2:30. He was shaky in the last case and didn't usually get that way until later in the day. He was irritable and I knew this was not going to be easy. As soon as I got the patient to recovery, I told him I needed to see him in his office. "I hope this doesn't take long. I'm busy", he barked as soon as I closed the door. "Randy, everyone here is worried about you" I started. He cut me off. "Don't bother giving me all your bullshit. I'm tired of hearing it." Now I was mad. "You will listen. You are a shadow of the man you used to be and the doctor you used to be. You treat everyone like shit and we are sick of it. Your work has gone down to the worst it's ever been and you don't care. You come in here bedraggled, unkempt, and crabby all the time. No one can even talk to you. You are short with the patients and you don't even call them anymore. You are hungover half the time and look it. We all know you are drinking and are wondering what else you are doing. You are getting scary." "Are you accusing me of being a drug addict?" he shouted. "You have a lot of fucking nerve. You know the stress I have been under. Maybe it is you who has been hacking my office. I always felt it was someone close. How dare you judge my surgical skill." His face was getting redder as he was shouting and he was out of his chair pacing. "You don't know anything about what I am going through. None of you do. All of you just care about your fat paychecks. I don't want anyone here that is not going to support me. I think you need to find another job. Give me 2 weeks to get other anesthesia in here and then get out. Since I am so scary, I'm sure you don't want to be around me." I tried again. "Randy all of us just want the real you back. This is not you. Be honest. You know your work has been off. We had 3 complications just this week. You never had issues before. Take some time off to get yourself under control. Go back to rehab for just a while. We know the stress you are under, but you are destroying yourself. We are lucky that the problems we have had were handled. It's too late once someone is really hurt. Please, Randy, just get help, however you can." Now he was enraged. "So, you are accusing me now of trying to kill my patients?" he screamed. "You fucking bitch. Miss holier than thou. Now I'm really convinced that you are behind all of the manipulations in my office. I will have new anesthesia in this office by the end of two weeks. You owe me to stay until then. I do not want to discuss this again. If you tell anyone else of your insane suspicions, I will sue you for defamation and make your life hell. Don't you dare turn any of my staff against me. Now get the fuck out of my office and leave me alone."

I walked out of his office and felt the tears flowing. I really struck out. However, I was not sorry that I told him the truth. I just wished I could have convinced him to take time off and help himself. Pam came up and gave me a silent hug. "I heard everything," she said. "I don't know what to do. Tom says I should resign. He thinks my being here enables him. But I think he would just hire someone else, and that would make the office even less safe for patients. What scares me is that it will take a really bad event before he accepts the truth." "I know, Pam. I have just reached a point where I can't be part of this". I told her about Mitch writing to the medical board members and our hope that maybe they could give some direction.

I left right away because I did not want to run into him again. I called Mitch and told him of my sad failure. "I'm not surprised, Sunny. He sees himself as getting by and dealing with his stress. He doesn't consider himself an addict. He's a time bomb, but you have to look out for yourself. I think all of you have been very loyal, but enough is enough. I sent the 2 letters today to the doctor's homes. I told them how worried we were and gave them my personal info. I said we were seeking direction for an intervention. I hope at least one will respond. I know he will blow up at me when he finds out, but I don't care. You know, he fired you. You are not obligated to stay until he gets new anesthesia. You could just not go back." "I know, Mitch, but I want to help whoever he hires to come in and get an orientation. That person will have their hands full with him. He has a seminar next week, so it will be 3 days and then the last week 4 days. I will stick it out".

I went home feeling really down. I made a drink and a snack and sat back rehashing the day. The doorbell rang and it was Teri. She was very upset. "I wanted you to know that I resigned," she said. I didn't know how much she had heard because she was in a different part of the facility when I was with Randy. "Jack has been wanting me to quit for the last couple of months. He's sick of me coming home angry and stressed out. I talked to Pam and told her I didn't want to deal with the whole situation anymore. He is impossible and an accident waiting to happen. Since he is getting new anesthesia, he can get a new RN too." I was surprised, but not much. I knew she had not been happy for a while. She only gave a week's notice and said Jack had a chance for a couple of weeks off, so they were taking it. Claudia knew the OR, so she would step into Teri's position as nurse supervisor and work between recovery and surgery. She knew a nurse for the OR and would help with orientation. Teri said she would help for the next week, but that was it. She had lost all respect for Randy and I understood. She had worked long hours and covered for him with patients many times. She was just done. We sat and talked for a couple of hours and shared our feelings. I suggested we all go to dinner on Saturday just to lift our spirits. We made it a foursome with Pam and Claudia and had a chance to vent and express our worries. We needed something to prepare us for the next couple of weeks. We all loved and missed the old Randy, but the current one was definitely on the edge. Pam admitted that she would probably be the last to go.

Claudia contacted Julia for the OR position. She interviewed on Monday and was hired. Then Pam gave me the bad news. Randy had hired new anesthesia and it was Bobby McFadden from the Hospital. His previous drug issues really had me worried. He was coming in next week for orientation with me.

It was a difficult week. Julia was very good, but not experienced in plastic surgery. Teri was very organized and that helped her a lot. There was an excellent policy and procedure manual. Randy was late every day, which had become his new normal. He looked terrible, but was trying hard to be pleasant to the staff. He was angry about the resignations, but deep down I know he knew why.

He did not speak to me, except regarding the patient. He snarled a few times, but I did not respond and we got through the days. Tuesday was especially stressful. He didn't arrive until 10:00 for his 8:00 case. The patient was angry and upset. Pam apologized, but she no longer covered for him with phony emergency excuses. When he did arrive, he looked hungover and unkempt. The patient's husband was outraged. He canceled his wife's surgery and demanded their money back. He told us he used to be an alcoholic and recognized how he used to drag himself into work. He called Randy a washed-up drunk. Randy said there was a no-return policy for cancellations on the day of surgery. The man got in his face and threatened to write a letter to the editor of the newspaper and do a negative review on social media. Pam convinced Randy to refund his money and get them out of the office. The next patient had arrived and she didn't want her upset. Randy took a shower, shaved and had a change of clothes. He looked much better, but was really shaken by the man's accusations. After the last case I took my patient to recovery and went back to clean up my anesthesia cart. Everything was gone. All my syringes were thrown away and the cart was wiped down. I called Teri. "Where is my equipment and syringes?" I asked. Before she could answer, Julia said "I'm used to doing it at the hospital, so I just threw out the syringes and took the equipment to be cleaned. I forgot that you like to clean up your own cart. I'm sorry". I told her it was okay, but to try to remember not to touch it. I had been watching my leftover Fentanyl and it upset me that I did not dispose of it myself. About a week ago a pan of Betadine got dumped on my tray at the end of the case. While I was in recovery with the patient, my cart was cleaned up. I did not see my Fentanyl syringe, so I was not sure what happened to it. That bothered me and now again today. I had no proof that Randy was taking any of my drugs, but the uncertainty really upset me.

Wednesday was more of the same. He was anxious to get finished and leave for his seminar. He was very hyped up and shaky by the time we finished. Pat told him she would close the breast incisions. He was so shaky that he was on his third attempt. As we were taking the patient out of the OR he came over and thanked Teri and wished her well. He looked much calmer and less shaky. All I could think about was the Fentanyl. Had he kept it or was I just paranoid? Maybe his paranoia was rubbing off on me. He still thought that I had something to do with the internet hacking. He came over to me. "Bobby is coming over one day next week after work. Will you show him around?" "Sure," I said. "I will be glad to give him an orientation". Those were the first civil words he had said to me since our blow-up. He was wearing a short sleeve shirt and I didn't see any evidence of needle marks. Maybe I was being paranoid, I thought. But in my heart, I was afraid. Afraid for him and his patients.

The long weekend was a fun break for me. Friday night I had dinner with Teri and Jack. She was going to take off for a month or two before deciding what to do next. She didn't want to go back to the hospital. The thought of the pace and taking call was too much. She said that Mitch had told her about the orthopedic center and she was considering it. Jack said he was glad that she was out of Randy's practice. "Something bad is going to happen sooner or later. I'm glad she finally listened to me." They were leaving over the weekend for vacation and looked happy.

Saturday was fun too. Mitch had arranged dinner with 2 of the ortho surgeons and their wives at one of the golf clubs where he was a member. He invited me and we had a great time. I liked all of them and they were pleased that I was considering joining their team. I said I wanted to take 2 weeks off and visit family. There were still some final steps before they would be credentialed and it would be at least a month. That was even better. I had a cousin in Seattle that I had not seen in a long time, so I would add that in. Mitch told me that he had not heard anything from either of the doctors on the board. Hopefully, they would come through with some advice soon.

Chapter 31

My last week was terrible. With Teri gone our routine was gone too. Claudia was in the OR for orientation with Julia and they tried hard. Pat was still new and she didn't have Teri to help her, so Monday and Tuesday were extremely slow. Randy was very impatient and griping at both of them. Pam convinced him to be on good behavior or he could end up with no staff. He had continued to arrive late, but Pat and Julia were glad. It gave them more time to prepare. Surgery afternoons were really stressful. He still got his afternoon lift, but would get shaky and very anxious to get through the cases. He cut corners to get the procedures done. After surgery, he would be in his office for a while and then come out calmer and much less anxious. I know he was drinking, but I didn't know what else he was doing. Wednesday, he saw patient consults.

On Thursday he was in a very dark mood. Two of the patients even asked if he was okay. Pam asked if he wanted to postpone a couple of cases. He snapped at her and then apologized. He said he had not been sleeping and that was why he was so short-tempered. He got his 3:00 perk up and was in a better frame of mind when Bobby came for his orientation. He was pleasant and said that he was looking forward to a change from the hospital. We finished the cases and I stayed late showing him the supplies and the paperwork. I got the narcotic keys and records and explained what drugs we used. I told him he could get other drugs, if there was something he preferred to use. He saw the Sufentanil and asked if I used it much. "Not a lot," I said, "but for certain patients it is superior to Fentanyl. I'm using it tomorrow in fact". "Why did you choose it," he asked. "One patient is a 30-year-old large man having a big liposuction. Some of these guys wake up wild and combative. With the Sufentanil they have better pain control and are much calmer and cooperative. It is 10 times stronger than Fentanyl and 100 times stronger than morphine." We discussed dosage and he said he had used it in orthopedic patients and really liked its effects. He hesitated a bit and then looked directly at me. "You know I had my own problems with Fentanyl a few years ago. It was really hard to beat that addiction. My wife has MS and I have 3 kids. They were the inspiration for me to get clean.

It wasn't easy and probably never will be." I was glad that he was being open and honest about his former addiction. "Bobby, if you feel anxious about the Fentanyl being right here, have Julia or Claudia get your drugs for you. You can share your history, if you choose. Just tell them to have the drugs ready when you do the count with them. Don't even take a key." "Thanks, Sunny. I'm going to do that. I can't go down that road again. I wouldn't even take this job, but the pay is really good and I get rid of call. Randy told me you are leaving because you wanted a change. He said you were going to an orthopedic center." I didn't know Randy knew or cared where I was going, but I didn't want to give Bobby any negative vibes. What if my suspicions somehow were wrong? He would find out for himself or Pam would fill him in as needed. I felt much more confident about Bobby. He was someone who had fought his demons and won. I wished him well and hoped this would work out for him.

I got home and was putting a salad together when I got a call from Mitch. "Be prepared" he said. "I got a call today from Bill, one of the docs on the medical board. He is very concerned about Randy and is coming here Tuesday to talk to him. He is meeting me in the afternoon and we hope you can come and share your concerns too. He and I are going to confront him at his office as soon as surgery is finished". "I am leaving for Seattle Wednesday afternoon, but I can meet you Tuesday. I am really glad that you got a response from someone who may be able to do something. I will meet you and Bill, but I'm not going to confront Randy again. He's been terrible to me and I can't take any more of his verbal tirades". "It's ok, Sunny. We will deal with him face to face. Bill just wants to hear your observations." I was glad of that. Tomorrow was my last day and it was going to be hard enough to get through. "What about the other doctor from the board? Did you hear from him?" "No, but Bill told me Isaac, the other doctor, called Randy and told him what I had written. Randy called me a little while ago screaming and threatening to sue me for defamation. He accused you and me of being in a conspiracy to destroy his practice. His paranoia is at an all-time high. I wanted to warn you to be prepared when you go in tomorrow." "I'm so glad that it is my last day. Thanks for the warning" I said.

I made up my mind to get through the last day as peacefully as I could, but I was not taking any more of his verbal abuse. As I was pulling in, I got a text from Pam. "Just a head up. He's waiting for you and he is steaming". I guess this will be the day from hell, I thought. I may as well get it over with. I barely got in the door and he was in my face. "My office. Now" and he stormed off. I went to his office and he started screaming. His face was red and he was shaking with rage. "I should have known it was you and Mitch behind everything that happened in this office. Now he has gotten the board of medicine involved. You lying bastards. I will sue you both." I had enough. I stood up and got right back in his face. "You are an alcoholic drug addict that is endangering patients. You know that I can barely get through paying my bills online, let alone put together a sophisticated online scheme. Mitch is as bad as I am on the internet. You want to blame someone because you won't look in the mirror and admit who is to blame. Yes, you were unfairly targeted, but you did not have to choose drugs and alcohol to deal with the problem. I have been nothing but supportive of you and I'm sick of your accusations. We have 2 big cases. Let's get them done, so I can get the hell away from you." This time I stormed off. "It can't be soon enough for me" he shouted as I closed the door.

Both patients were large men and I planned to use Sufentanil for both of them. It really helped with post-op pain. The first one was ultrasonic liposuction of the abdomen, flanks, and back. Randy complained about everything the whole case. He picked at Pat and Julia over every trivial issue. Claudia tried to help, but it was impossible. When the case finished Pat told him that she needed a lunch break. "All you think about is food" he snarked. "We don't need a break". She looked him in the eye and said "I will take my lunch break or I will leave and you can do the last case yourself. I need a break from your bitching". Just then Pam's assistant came to the door and told him he had a phone call. He stomped off and slammed his door. "Good for you, Pat," I told her. She laughed. "I grew up in a house with my dad and 4 boys. I don't take crap. If he doesn't like it, he can fire me. He would be doing me a favor, but I would miss the money." Julia was still getting used to the place and looked nervous. His tirades were very upsetting.

We finally started our last case. It was a big liposuction with the excision of loose skin. Randy was less agitated but already shaky, and I noticed he was sweating. The patient was large and the case tedious. He told Julia to get a new gown and gloves for him because he was taking a quick break. That was unusual. He never left a case. He broke scrub and went to his office. He was gone for about 10 minutes, then rescrubbed and gowned. He seemed calmer. I asked him if he was ok. "What the hell do you care?" he said. Ok, I thought. Just a few more hours to go. There was more than usual bleeding with the liposuction. He accused Claudia of not telling the patient to stop aspirin and ibuprofen. "No, Dr. Tanner, I did tell him and I gave him written instructions too." He started the skin excision and the bleeding was worse. It was coming from the liposuction area. A blood vessel may have been injured by the liposuction cannula and he was having trouble finding the bleeder. He would have to extend the incision so he could visualize the vessel. He told Claudia to scrub in so she could hold retractors. He was sweating again and shakier. Claudia scrubbed in and was able to get him better visibility. It took a while, but he found the bleeder.

He was so shaky, that he had trouble tying the vessel off. I breathed a sigh of relief when I saw it was under control. Claudia broke scrub and went back to recovery to warm more fluids and blankets. Pam's assistant came to the door holding a large manila envelope. "Dr. Tanner," she said. "There was a courier who came by and left this envelope for you. It was not in the mail, just a private courier." "What the hell do you want me to do about it?" he barked. "Can't you see I'm busy? Put it on my desk and go away".

The surgery was almost finished. I turned off the anesthesia and was giving extra fluid. What a stressful procedure. Randy was really sweating and shaky. I think the fact that he had not been able to quickly control the bleeding had frightened him. I hoped so. He grabbed a clean sponge from the OR table and mopped his face and neck. He threw the sponge on the floor and cursed at Pat and Julia, telling them how slow and incompetent they were. "I'm taking a break after I get the patient to recovery," I told him. "I will get my things out of here after." "Suit yourself," he said sarcastically. "Just get your crap and get out. I never want to see you again." I saw his quick glance at my anesthesia tray. "Randy, I used Sufentanil on the patients today. Not Fentanyl". "I don't care what you used. Just get the hell out of here" he yelled over his shoulder as he went to his office. The patient was awakening and we went to the recovery room to get him warm and comfortable.

I came back to clean up my anesthesia cart and was upset to see it empty again. "Julia, did you throw away my anesthesia supplies?" I asked. "I'm so sorry, Sunny, I did. He had me so upset all day that I just didn't think and threw everything away." "Did you notice if my Sufentanil syringe was on the tray?" I asked. "No. I just grabbed all the syringes and threw them in the sharp's box." Damn, I thought. I told him, but I would have liked to dispose of it myself.

Randy went to recovery to check on the patient. He was glad to see he was awake and stable. What a case it had been. If I had better help, it would have been easier to find that bleeder he thought. Bobby was coming in next week for anesthesia. Maybe I need to switch to a male staff. These damn women and their whining and bullshit were getting to be too much. He planned to push even harder to do more cases. If he changed staff maybe all of this internet harassment would go away. He went to his office and poured a generous single malt. That would help. He pulled the leftover syringe from my tray out of his pocket and changed the needle. There wasn't a lot left, but that was fine. All he needed was a little bump to calm down and control the shakes. He got the tourniquet out and then noticed the manila envelope. That's odd he thought. Just his name with no return address. He sipped more scotch and was beginning to feel calmer. He opened the envelope and was surprised to find a small book. No letter or anything else. He looked at the cover and it said "Laura's Diary". Who was Laura and why am I getting this? He flipped through a few pages and became aware that this had belonged to Laura Devon. What the hell? He polished off the scotch and noticed there were a few pages paper clipped together. The marked pages started with the time he had taken Laura to the frat party. He was stunned about the pregnancy and the abortion. As he read about her hopelessness and suicide, it dawned on him. Charlie. Fucking Charlie had been the one destroying his life and now he was livid. Laura had not told him, so what was he supposed to do? None of it was his fault because he didn't know. I am going to sue him and make him pay for what he has put me through. He was really agitated and now he needed that bump more than ever.

I had everything in the anesthesia supply area in order and had written a long note to Bobby. I encouraged him to contact me if he had any questions. I looked around and felt empty. We had all been so excited about this new practice just 3 years ago. Randy was blessed with good looks, a charismatic personality and exceptional surgical talent. I watched it all slip away and couldn't help the tears of sadness. The patient was discharged and everyone had left, but I was still worried about the Sufentanil. I stopped at Randy's office and knocked on the door. "What?" he shouted. I was relieved to hear his voice. "Goodbye, Randy, and good luck. I just wanted to remind you that I used Sufentanil on the patients today." "Go away, Sunny. You are nothing to me anymore". Stupid bitch, he thought, rambling on about her drugs. He couldn't stop thinking about Charlie and wondered why he hadn't just called him and told him about Laura. I'm sure he was jealous of me too. He is not going to get away with this and his mind was racing with ideas of revenge. I have to relax and think straight, he thought. The tourniquet was in place and he slipped the tiny needle into his vein. He injected slowly and felt it immediately. A thought came to his mind as his eyes closed and his body became so heavy that he could not move. Did Sunny say Sufentanil? Is that what she was yapping about?

As I walked to my car, I saw Wes coming in for the terminal cleaning. "Hi Wes" I called. "Hi Sunny. I heard you are leaving. Good luck to you". "Thanks, Wes. By the way, Randy said he wanted to talk to you. He's in his office". "OK, I'll see him first thing". I felt better knowing that Wes would give a final check on him. As I drove away, I couldn't stop the tears. I hated leaving this way and the fact that I could not help Randy. In my heart I knew my future was bright. I am a CRNA and I can give anesthesia anywhere. I love my work and my patients and there would be new opportunities ahead. Randy had a gift of great surgical ability and I hoped he would find the strength to rescue it. I didn't notice the sirens in the background.

ACKNOWLEDGMENT

For over 28 years I had the good fortune to work with a group of talented and dedicated nurse anesthetists. We provided ambulatory in-office anesthesia service to 26 accomplished and expert plastic surgeons in central Florida. I thank all of them for my wonderful career. Thanks are not complete without mentioning the most important people- my patients. This book is a work of fiction, including the facilities and the physicians. The patient scenarios are based on my real surgical patients, who were always interesting and colorful. I loved them all and hope you enjoy reading about them.

There are some people that I want to give a special thanks for their input and direction. First to Peter and his team for their excellent publishing guidance. And then to all the family and friends that supported me, including Tom, Pam, Charity, Michael, Jay, Terry, Laura, Gary, Pat, Julia, Lori and Adrienne. Most of all, I give a very special thanks to you, the reader. I hope you enjoyed reading this as much as I enjoyed writing it.

www.ingramcontent.com/pod-product-compliance
Lightning Source LLC
Chambersburg PA
CBHW040900010826
48978CB00013BA/1099